THE CAULDRON

Kueli had died shrieking his fear of it—Bran's warriors had seen its baleful glow on the ramparts of besieged Tara—and now they faced the full power of its dire sorcery.

For in an ill hour Bran had gifted Matholuch with the Cauldron of Re-birth, stolen long ago from the Gods—and Matholuch, desperate in defeat, had turned to the Cauldron for help.

With the dawn, the Irish attacked again—but this time with an unconquerable army spawned by the Cauldron—an army of the risen dead!

By *Evangeline Walton*:

THE BOOKS OF THE WELSH MABINOGION
Published by Ballantine Books

PRINCE OF ANNWN
From the First Branch

THE CHILDREN OF LLYR
From the Second Branch

THE SONG OF RHIANNON
From the Third Branch

THE ISLAND OF THE MIGHTY
From the Fourth Branch

The Children of Llyr

by

Evangeline Walton

The Second Branch of the Mabinogion

A Del Rey Book

BALLANTINE BOOKS • NEW YORK

A Del Rey Book
Published by Ballantine Books

ISBN 0-345-27738-4

Manufactured in the United States of America

First Edition: August 1971
Fifth Printing: December 1978

Cover art by Howard Koslow

*To that great Welsh-born man of letters,
the late John Cowper Powys,
Whom the author never met,
but without whose written interest and
encouragement this book might never
have been written.*

Contents

On Evangeline Walton—and Magic

(from "The Saturday Review" by Patrick Merla)

———————

". . . The essential element of any true work of fantasy is magic—a force that affects the lives and actions of all the creatures that inhabit the fantasist's world. This magic may be innate or manifest; it may be used by the characters who live with it, or come from 'gods' of the author's contrivance. Always it is a *supernatural* force whose use, *mis*use, or *dis*use irrevocably changes the lives of those it touches.

. . . Now, magic is like religion and politics: few people agree about it. . . . I believe in magic. Not as mystic mumbo jumbo, but as a way of life. . . . Having long been a student of mysticism (Oriental and Occidental), I have observed that a magical substructure underlies the best fantasies. A book's setting may be Khendiol (*Red Moon and Black Mountain*), King Arthur's England (*The Once and Future King*), or ancient Wales (*The Mabinogion*), but its magic is Real Magic, an archetypal life-giving quality, consistent with magic as it has always been. (In a way this 'cosmic uniformity' is similar to the astonishing similarity of the poetry of Kabir, Rumi, and St. John of the Cross—three mystics from different eras and cultures, all of whom wrote about their religious experiences in almost identical terms.)

There are as many ways of enjoying fantasy books as

there are volumes. A comparison of works derived in some way from *The Mabinogion* (The Druidic books of legends of the Welsh people)—both from a literary standpoint and as magical expositions—may give readers an idea of the nature of successful fantasy.

J. R. R. Tolkien and Joy Chant have both made use of magical archetypes found in *The Mabinogion* to enrich their own books; Evangeline Walton's books, on the other hand, are actual retellings of these diverse legends in novel form. Each of these works deals with the struggle between the forces of Good and Evil. Each of them presents some form of quest. Three of them deal with the nature of love.

. . . Not even Tolkien can create names more magical than those found in *The Mabinogion* itself. (Of course, the Druids were wielders of Real Magic.) In one sense, therefore, Evangeline Walton had some of her work already done for her before she began to write her tetralogy based on the four 'branches' of *The Mabinogion*. These books, together with C. S. Lewis's *Out of the Silent Planet, Perelandra,* and *That Hideous Strength* and T. H. White's *The Once and Future King,* are not only the best fantasies of the twentieth century. They are also great works of fiction.

. . . The wonders of Walton's books are manifold. . . . I suspect that Evangeline Walton knows something about magic from personal experience. Her books are so thoroughly steeped in mysticism that mere anthropological knowledge of Druidical lore is insufficient to explain their authority. Only C. S. Lewis has matched Walton's subtle depiction of the forces of Good and Evil.

. . . Walton succeeds in creating an imaginary world that we believe *actually existed* in this world's history. She is able to do what few writers of worth would dare attempt: to predict a future we have already witnessed —this century's wars—and to make that prediction credible in the context of the past she presents.

In Walton's realm of Gwynedd magic does not disappear when materialism enters the scene—as it does in Tolkien's book and in most of the works drawn from

The Mabinogion. It merely becomes invisible to men who would not wish to see it if they could. . . ."

The Beginning

Llyr Llediaith was a Chief among the Old Tribes, and the woman he slept with was black-haired Penardim, Penardim who was beautiful. Her brother was Beli of the Deep, High-King over all the Island of the Mighty. Even the New Tribes paid him tribute, the fierce invaders from beyond the sea.

But Beli ruled by the law of the Old Tribes. When his time came he would choose his heir from among his sister's sons—his nephews, the sons of Penardim and Llyr.

Penardim did not call Llyr husband, nor did her children call him father. The Old Tribes had no such words. Easy to imagine a young man scratching his head and saying, "Yes, I know, Grandmother. But the New Tribes say that their girls do not have children till after . . ."

"The New Tribes! Impertinent good-for-nothings! It is not that easy to make a woman's belly swell. Children are the gifts made to women by the Mothers, by the ancient Powers that bring spring and summer. Their beginning is among the Mysteries."

"Yes, but . . ."

"And as for those girls of the New Tribes, I know them! And so do you! It is not because they do not have men that they do not have children before they have husbands."

And the young man would grin and remember (or pretend to if he did not), and say that that was so. Besides, a child certainly was not made every time a man lay with a woman. At that rate any brisk young fellow ought to get dozens every moon. Better to leave such matters to the Gods; a man should not presume too far.

So it was when Llyr Llediaith and Penardim the King's sister came together, and to them man and woman meant only Llyr and Penardim. All others were but sexless, secondary shapes floating outside the rich warm island of being that was these two. So it was among these two when Llyr made the circuit of the land to collect tribute for Beli; when he came to the house of Eurosswydd mab Maelgwn, a chief among the New Tribes, and stopped there.

Taxes are seldom paid gladly, and no tax collector could have been less welcome to Eurosswydd than Llyr. Between these two dislike was somehow as inevitable as between fire and water. Llediaith means "Half-Speech," for Llyr spoke the Island tongue brokenly; he had come from the mainland, where the New Tribes were triumphant, and his memories were bitter. Yet he had many friends among the New Tribes; only when he looked at Eurosswydd did he remember how this man's people had fallen upon his with fire and sword. And whenever Eurrosswydd saw Llyr he thought, *None ever forget that my grandfather and his folk were not born here. Yet although this man himself was born elsewhere, he has got many more friends than I have, both among his people and mine. He has got the King's own ear. He has got the King's sister.*

Thinking thus, he felt himself unjustly made small, and the idea of paying taxes to Llyr made him feel smaller, and he was a man who liked to feel large. So he drank too much, and in the end he pounded on the table, and refused to pay.

"For my father Maelgwn pledged taxes to Beli, and to Beli I will pay them, but I am no man of yours, Llyr Llediaith, to pay you anything at all!"

"I am sent by Beli," said Llyr, "and all I get I must give account of to Beli. When he asks for what is lacking, shall I tell him that Eurosswydd, Maelgwn's son, withheld it?"

"Tell him why I withheld it," said Eurosswydd, "and that to himself I will pay it."

"What if he comes after it?" said Llyr, and his voice was soft, as the fur of a pouncing cat is soft.

Beli might not have come in war. His dignity was too high to be above patience, and his lifework had been the welding of friendship between Old Tribes and New. Llyr did wrong to make threats so soon. But the hot fumes that he kept out of his face and voice seethed round his brain.

They flashed out of Eurosswydd like sparks out of a smitten anvil. His voice leapt at Llyr like a beast. "Then he may get it, and my head with it, but it is not you who will get steward's fees out of it, stumbling-tongued outlander!"

Then his voice too grew soft, but as rotten fruit is soft, and he said, "Yet why let you go to babble lying tales to Beli?"

Llyr saw the spear at his throat then. In that banquet hall Eurosswydd had three men to each of his. But his face did not change and his voice was as cool as ever as he said, "Death is a fair woman, Eurosswydd; or so some say. But are you so much in love with her that you would throw yourself into her arms for the pleasure of pushing me into them first?"

"By my hand," swore Eurosswydd, "it is not into the arms of any woman I wanted that I ever would push you! I am a man—I keep my women to myself. Not like you honorless bastards, you half-men, that come when you are called and go when you are bidden, obedient as puppy dogs to your women's lusts! Women! I know a better name for them." He spat as he said it. "I would take a whip to all their backs—these strutting sluts of your Old Tribes—and teach them what a man is. They would soon forget you puppy dogs!"

All round the hall there was a bright flicker of swords—the snick of one being drawn wherever a man of the Old Tribes was. But Llyr raised his hand, empty, and all the swords fell.

"You have refused Beli's tribute to Beli's officer," he said quietly, and his eyes pinned Eurosswydd. "In the morning, when your mind speaks, and not the wine in your belly, you may think better of that. If you do not, I will go down to the ford and fight you there. So shall our men go unharmed, and the quarrel be between us, and nothing to Beli."

His eyes did not turn from Eurosswydd's nor relax their spearlike fixity until the red angry eyes of Maelgwn's son fell.

Eurosswydd said low and sullenly, "So be it. But you will not come back alive from the ford, Llyr."

"That is as may be," said Llyr. "Let us eat."

But upon that feast had fallen a gloomy silence. Like a black bird it perched upon each man's shoulder. All ate, but none tasted his food. The bards harped, but their harping brought no beauty to birth; it only made a noise that seemed afraid of silence.

Llyr thought, *I have come to a fertile field, and*

I have sown bad seed—the kind it was fittest to grow. Will I get my men and myself out of this alive? And if I do, how have I served Beli whom I talked so loudly of serving?

His men and Eurosswydd's were thinking too, thoughts as like as twins: *Had we better sleep with our swords on? There may be treachery in these Other Tribe folk. There is bound to be—they have always stunk with it. But if we sleep armed, they may say we planned to rise and slay them in their sleep. Make that their excuse . . .*

Their thoughts turned red and they mused, *It would be good to rise up and slay these Other Tribe folk now and let their blood run out. Then we could sleep in peace.*

Eurosswydd sat still, and looked at the long red hairs that grew, grass-thick, upon his hands. He was unhappy. He was ashamed, because he glared at his own hands and feet, and not at Llyr. *Was it by magic that he made my eyes fall? The Old Tribes are strong in magic . . .*

In his mind he saw the ford, and the cold gray of dawn.

He said angrily in his heart, *Magic will not help him now. I will carve him as a side of beef is carved.* His mind drew joyous pictures of that carving and the accompanying bloodletting. He felt free and powerful and happy, certainly the better man. He saw himself a hero; to follow him the New Tribes would rise to a man. *I will set Llyr's head upon one of my doorposts, and Beli's on the other.* Until a voice whispered, a small cold voice in the back of his own head, *But what if his magic prevails over your strength? As it made your eyes fall . . .*

He tried to think that hand-to-hand, Llyr could not do magic. But he could not feel sure; one could not be sure, with a magician. He thought angrily, *It is not fair.* All along Llyr had outwitted him, goading him to fight, cleverly robbing him of the advantage of superior numbers. It had seemed fair and chieftain-like, that offer of single combat, so chieftain-like that he could not turn it down before his men. But if it was not—if it was not—if Llyr counted on magic to spit him like a sheep . . .

He thought, *Guile is fair against guile,* and again, *He sleeps in my house tonight.*

If Llyr had slept anywhere else, Eurosswydd could have waited honorably enough for morning. He would have thought his face lost forever if he had not gone down to the ford. But now every moment seemed like a spear that lay in his hand and that time twisted from him, saying as it passed, *"This is gone, and you have not used it. You fool, who sit here waiting for him who lolls in your own hall, full of your meat, to slay you by craft."*

Faster and faster time twisted them from him, those precious bright minutes. Like gold falling from a bag's mouth into the sea.

Gold that might well be his own lifeblood . . .

His mind began to work. It was the part of him least used to exercise, and it burrowed molelike, scurrying here and there in dark, crooked passages.

He called a bard to him, a man whose mother's kin were druids, but whom the Old Tribes had cast out for some crime. He whispered to that man, whose eyes grew narrow and bright.

"I can do it, Lord. But there will be none to help you when it is done, for the charm falls upon all alike. You yourself had best go quickly from the hall."

Eurosswydd said, "Make me a sign when the danger comes."

"I cannot, Lord. The charm will take all of me. But not long will you be safe, staying."

He went back to his harp and sang. That song was a marvel and a mystery. It was sweeter than honey, more monotonous than a daylong fall of rain. It was softer than those lowest notes of lullabies that are lost in the throats of mothers; sweet shadows of sound. It was the distilled essence of all sleep; it was the shadow of death.

Weariness came upon the feasters. Mist gathered before their eyes, their lids grew heavy as stones. They slid from their places limply, grotesquely, legs rising and arms falling, like dolls dropped by children. Only Eurosswydd, stumbling, lurched out of the hall while the others fell. Like brothers his men slept beside Llyr's; beside Llyr himself.

The torches guttered out, untended, and night, no longer held at bay, crept in softly through the doors and took back this one tiny nest of rebels. Wrapped them all in the vast, gentle cloak of her blackness . . .

The sun came and burned that dark coverlet away, and still the men lay there; only now Llyr's were weaponless, and heavy thongs bound their arms and legs. Like flies caught in the web of some coarse giant spider they lay there. The men of Eurosswydd still slept beside them. But the bard sat smiling broadly, a new gold chain about his neck. The slaves who had been called to bind the sleeping guests had all gone back to their huts.

Eurosswydd the son of Maelgwn sat and looked at his captives, and the mole in his head worked on.

To kill Llyr now would mean outlawry. His honor would go out with his foe's life, like a torch in a fetid pool. For Llyr had been a guest in his house, and never could he prove to any, not even quite to himself, that Llyr would have used magic at the ford.

Yet Llyr the Prisoner was also Llyr the Hostage—they would swear Eurosswydd peace, those chiefs of the Old Tribes, they would give him gold and lands to get Llyr out of his hands alive and whole. And Llyr himself would walk a shamed man forever after, memories burning him like whip weals. Oh, but he should have memories! Before he went free he would know who was master. Llyr the Very Proud, the father of the King that would be!

The King that would be! Penardim's boys were Beli's heirs. That pride never could be taken from Llyr. His seed would lord it over the New Tribes in days to come.

Over my own children, whatever vengeance I take.

Like lightning a thought struck Eurosswydd. Like a fresh log falling upon the fires within him. It flared up in a blaze that dazzled his mole brain . . .

He laughed and pounded his chair with his fists. His eyes shone as he called the smiling bard; their pupils were like little murky fires dancing evilly in the reddened whites.

"You are the only man of mine that is yet awake. You will bear my words to Penardim the sister of Beli. To Llyr's woman . . ."

He spoke these words, and the man heard them and trembled, but he had to repeat them after his Lord. His little time of power and praise was over.

Not happily the bard came before Penardim, in her house, where she waited the sister of Llyr.

She was tall, the sister of Beli. Her hair glistened like blackbirds' feathers; her high sweet breasts, still girlishly erect, the pure lines of her head and body made music. She was like a torch shining in a dark quiet place. She was straight as a torch, cleanly and beautifully made.

"You bring me tidings from Llyr Llediaith?"

"Not from, but of him, Lady. He stopped at the house of my master Eurosswydd, and he is a prisoner there."

She quivered once, as if beneath a sudden blow. Then her face became hard as stone; colder than stone.

"Llyr was not easily taken. By what treachery?"

"Lady," he stammered, licking pale lips, "Lady, there was a quarrel. The Lord Llyr made magic with his eyes, and struck my master dumb in his own hall. But in the household of Eurosswydd is a man who has this quality—he can sing a song that will put sleep upon the worst-wounded man, upon the most fevered and pain-torn. That man sang the Song of Sleep to Llyr and his comrades, and they were disarmed and bound."

He shrank. He hoped that she would think that man far away, yet feared that she would not. All his thoughts seemed like fish swimming in clear water, bared to her gaze.

She saw them but did not think of him. She faced the need to save; she would not yet face the need to avenge.

"Your master has Llyr," she said, "and presently Beli my brother will have him. Has he thought about that?"

"He has, Lady. Many days will pass before Beli who is in Arvon can gather the Cantrevs and march to my master's house. By then he can be safe in Gaul or Ireland with chiefs who will give great gifts to him who can show them where and how best to ravage Beli's coasts. He gives you this day and this night to decide in—whether you will pay him Llyr's ransom, or he shall send you Llyr's head."

"How much?" Her voice that was cold as snow bargained; she was a good housewife.

He looked at the ground. He looked at her shoes, and tried to count the stitches on them.

"Well?" she said.

He tried to answer; he opened his mouth, but it worked only soundlessly. Death was the least of his fears now. He was remembering much that in Eurosswydd's house he had half forgotten: the powers of her ancient royal line that was younger only than the Gods. The might that not only could sweep him from the earth, but bring him back to it as a mouse or a beetle or some yet more lowly thing.

Perhaps even unself him, make him nothing . . .

At last he got sound out; it was low and quavery, but it was sound. He had no power to keep back one word, to plead, or evade, or soften. "Lady, he asks this: that you come to his house and mate with him. In the morning both you and Llyr may go unharmed. By the sun and by the moon he swears it, and by the vigor of his body, that he would have you taste."

The druids came to her in her Sunny Chamber. Tall men with white robes and beards, and in their hands the wands that were said to have power to put upon a man the shape of bird or beast.

They said, "Lady, wait. A man in battle does not throw away his shield, and Llyr is Eurosswydd's shield."

She said, "You are wrong. He has boasted that he will take Llyr's head off and he will do it; he would be afraid not to. He is a small man trapped in his own big words, and there is nothing more dangerous than that."

"There is, Lady. There are dark beings that lurk between the worlds, seeking bodies and birth. Often such have been born into the Eastern World, tyrants and torturers. But here where we live under the Ancient

Harmonies, simple folk still close to the Mothers, no woman's body has yet been a door to let them in."

"You speak of the Mysteries," said Penardim, "and I revere the Mysteries. But it is my man I am thinking about now. Not to escape one night's misery will I lie all the nights of my life without Llyr by my side. No—I have borne children, and though this is worse than childbirth, like that it will pass."

Her women were there, and one of them said, "Llyr himself may not like it, Lady."

"Where a woman of our people sleeps, and with whom, is for her to say. So it always has been, and so it always will be. I am not giving away lands or goods of my man's, that he might ask account of if he were fool enough to want to die for them. Nor would Llyr wish Beli my brother to lose men and slay men for his sake."

"If Llyr and his slayers and avengers do not die, many more men may," said the eldest druid. "Go, women." And they went swiftly, shivering.

But Penardim sat and faced him, and her eyes were steady. "You need not have sent my women away. They know as well as I do that I may bear a child to Eurosswydd. Have not you wise druids learned that most women know that much nowadays? Maybe all women that have loved a man much. Could I doubt it, who see what Llyr must have looked like, and he little, every time I see my Manawyddan's face?"

"Would you give him a monster for brother, woman?"

"Strong words, druid. I will count it bad enough if I bring forth another Eurosswydd, and he is no monster. He is too small for that. And indeed, I think that, whoever else dies, he will soon be smaller by a head."

"Lady, well you know that all lovers are strings of

a mighty harp. All that live, man and woman, bird and beast, the fish undersea and the snake that crawls through the deep grasses, all make that music. No woman of the Old Tribes ever yet has sought a man and conceived his child save when it sang through her being. That music is life's source and love's delight. It is the one chance of man and woman to be as Gods and to fashion breathing life. You who would go to a man you hate, who seeks you only for spite—will you open the door of your body to what may come?"

She said, "I cannot let Llyr die. And as for my child, who knows in what image it may be fashioned? I will close my mind against the Red Man. I will see only Llyr—think only of Llyr."

"You are a strong woman," said the druid, "but you will not be able to do that. Not all through the night . . ."

She looked past him. She looked through the walls and the waning light; and with her heart's eyes she looked into the face of Llyr, that shone warm and clear. Her own face was as set as her will; again a face carved in stone.

She said, "I will not let Llyr die. The Island of the Mighty must take its chance with my child—the child that may never be born."

In the red of that sunset she began her journey. And the winds bared their knives and the leaves moaned and shuddered beneath their cold bite. The whole Island of the Mighty shivered in the grip of descending night.

The druid stood and watched distance take her.

He watched longer, while darkness piled up about him like smoke, and what he watched only himself knew, and perhaps not even the mind of him; there may be that in man which goes where mind cannot follow. He drew his cloak about him and shivered beneath those biting winds.

"So be it," he said, "since so it must be. Night falls now, a World Night, and a dark age draws on. The end of all we have known, the beginning of the new. Well, so long as all be part of the Great Going-Forward, so long as good comes again at last, rising out of evil."

So began the journey of Penardim the Dark Woman, the mother of the sons of Llyr.

She came to the House of Eurosswydd, and the housefolk welcomed her with so many torches that the path to his door seemed as though lined with fallen stars.

Eurosswydd met her there, before his door. He laughed his high neighing laugh and flung out his arms; he gave her the host's kiss of greeting, and she gave it back again.

She went into his hall and ate with him, and later she went to his bed. She stood beside it and unfastened the brooches that held her robe; and it seemed to her that no deed in the world ever had taken so long or been so slow. She felt like a bowman who had been standing rigid, cramped, for hours, every thought and nerve and muscle fixed on keeping his arrow aimed, his arm steady.

On not relaxing, not letting go . . .

Beside her Eurosswydd was stripping his broad, hairy body. The red bristles on it made her think of a pig's back she once had seen; hunters had carried it in from the forest, the carcass swinging on a pole. But the pig had been cold; Eurosswydd's body would be horribly warm . . . *Do not feel, do not think, except of Llyr!*

Only tonight, only this one night! Tomorrow night, and for all the nights to come, Llyr again, only Llyr!

*He will not be here long, this other, you will not have
to grip yourself like this long, not to see him, to keep
him out. Be strong. Oh, be far away, that which is I!*

She felt his hands, hot upon her body, upon her
breasts. She felt his kisses, hot and wet and sickening.
He was laughing, pulling her down onto the bed—
and suddenly something inside her shrank and scurried
back, sick, into the innermost recesses of herself.

*He cannot enter you. Your flesh is not you; it is
a garment that you have not always had and that will
be replaced . . . No! O Mothers, no!*

*Leave the body there upon the bed; let him have
it. You are separate from that; you must be. You must
stay away, hiding in some inner space, clinging to
Llyr . . . See only Llyr, think only of Llyr. Oh, be
very far away!*

In the morning they both went to the place where
Llyr lay bound. With eyes like colored stones he looked
up at them, eyes emptied of all feeling, carefully, fiercely blank. He saw how white and drawn Penardim's face
was, her eyes tired and sunken. He saw Eurosswydd's
grin.

The Red Man strode to Llyr and stood over him.
His grin widened until it seemed like the sky. Immense, inescapable; it covered the world.

"You are not the only man who has fathered a
nephew of Beli's, Llyr. Not if I know my strength,
and I never put in a night to better purpose—by the
Gods, this will be a fine tale to tell! How Llyr Llediaith
came to my house and slept so hard that he could not
get out again until his woman came and slept with
me—a livelier sleeping time that!" He threw back his
head and shook with laughter. Like thunder it rolled,
and the room shook with him.

Penardim knelt by Llyr. As she cut his hands free

she said, "I have paid dear for your life, Llyr. Do not make that go for nothing."

Eurosswydd still laughed, but his face turned a slow, blotched crimson. Llyr's was as white as death.

"This is his time for talking, woman; let him do it. Now cut these ropes round my legs."

"Not so fast," said Eurosswydd. "First you must promise not to stir up Beli against me."

Llyr looked straight into his eyes and calmly. "I will pledge you Beli's peace, but not my own."

"Beli's is good enough for me," said Eurosswydd; and chuckled.

But there was little heart in that chuckle. His vanity was bleeding; he had hoped to make a good impression on the woman. Also those two still stood together and against him, as if in some druid circle that he could not enter. He kept reminding himself that that was not true; he had had the woman.

He got no happiness out of the memory of that morning save for that one sudden blanching of Llyr's face.

And on a day in autumn, when frost had turned the trees to marvels of gold and fire, his own face blanched. For Llyr rode with his own men out of his own land, and spears ringed round the house that had heard the Song of Sleep.

Llyr spoke to those within through a trumpet, and this is what he said. "Come out, Eurosswydd, and we two will go down to the ford at last. Come out, and I will let your folk go free."

Eurosswydd did not want to go. But there were too many eyes on him; there had been too much talk about the trickery he had used before. He was afraid his own men might think him a coward. He raked together the faggots of his pride and kindled them to a final blaze. In savage and nervous hope he went down to the ford.

He went farther than that.

He went out of his body and out of the Island of the Mighty, and that was the end of him, there and elsewhere. For wherever he is now he is not Eurosswydd, any more than an oak is the acorn from which it sprang. Arawn, Lord of the Underworld, judged him and no doubt melted up most of him, yet saved the little that was good enough to be used again.

He went and men forgot him, because he had not been memorable; also he had gone in fair fight, so that neither New Tribes nor Old need hold a grudge.

Except for two reasons, his very name long ago would have been forgotten, but because of those two it never can be so long as the Island of the Mighty remembers the tongue of its youth. A few moons after he died Penardim bore those two, and they were her sons and his. Nissyen and Evnissyen were their names.

Three winters passed, and spring came again, and when the land was fragrant with blossoms she bore another child—Branwen, daughter of Llyr.

1

The Coming of the Stranger

Bran, first son of Llyr and Penardim, was King over all the Island of the Mighty. In Llwndrys, later to be called London, his name had been cried, and there he had been crowned.

Pwyll of Dyved must have seen that crowning, he who reigned among the New Tribes with Rhiannon, the Queen who had come to him out of Faery, though well she knew that age and death must be the price of her love for him. Math, son of Mathonwy, must have seen it, that avatar who was called the Ancient. In many bodies he had ruled over the people of Gwynedd, the pure stock of the Old Tribes, and would rule them until the time came for both him and them to change. That time was drawing near. His successor was already born, his sister's son, Gwydion, son of Don.

If those two chiefs said yea to Bran's crowning, none could say nay, though Caswallon, son of Beli, may have watched with secret, dreaming eyes . . .

Bran the Blessed he was called, for he was kind

17

and just, and in his time every cow that calved twinned, and every field and orchard bore double. But his woman died young, and he kept her only child, and called the boy Caradoc, son of Bran. People were not so surprised as they once would have been. Belief in fatherhood was growing; nobody could quite forget that there was some difference between the children of Penardim. Between the children of Llyr and the sons of red Eurosswydd.

On a day when young Caradoc mab Bran was in his teens the court was camped upon the Rock of Harlech. Bran sat there looking down upon the shores of Merioneth, and in the mists that rose up from the sea his great form looked like that great rock's topmost crag and pinnacle. He was mightily made, the biggest of the sons of men. The *Mabinogi* says that no house or ship could hold him, though if that tale has not grown in the telling, houses and ships must have been small then. One thing only seems certain: Bran was very big.

Two of his mother's sons, Manawyddan mab Llyr and Evnissyen mab Eurosswydd, were with him there, and so was Caradoc, his own son. Caradoc was playing with a golden ball, throwing it up into the air and catching it as it came down again. Evnissyen eyed that game with disfavor, as he soon did all sports in which nothing was killed or maimed.

"You will be a long time hitting the sky at that rate, boy. You have not come anywhere near the lowest cloud yet."

Caradoc missed the ball then; it fell, and Evnissyen chuckled. The boy turned, saying in a voice that was sharper than he meant it to be, "I am not trying to hit anything, uncle. And why should anybody be fool enough to try to hit the sky?"

Evnissyen grinned. "Myself, I would rather aim at

something than at nothing, but maybe it is as well that you lack ambition, young one. In the south young Pryderi will be king in Dyved after his father Pwyll, but you, the High-King's own son, will be lucky to get one or two miserable Cantrevs. Branwen's sons will king it after Bran, not you."

Manawyddan said peaceably, "Dyved is a little kingdom, brother, such as could easily pass under the New Tribes, and so from father to son. But Caradoc here is what no man in the Island of the Mighty ever was before—the High-King's acknowledged son. Caswallon and his brothers always have had to be content with saying that Beli was the man their mother slept with."

Evnissyen promptly became very fond of Caradoc. Threefold opportunity dazzled him—to forgive and defend Caradoc, who had snapped at him, and yet at the same time thoroughly to annoy both his brother and his nephew. He pounced on it as a cat pounces on a mouse.

"Well, it is nice to be able to boast of one's high descent, but it would be nicer still to have what goes with it—the fruit as well as the rind. But then I too might praise Caradoc's lack of ambition, Manawyddan, if I were in your shoes. They are a good place to be, since Branwen is staying a virgin remarkably long."

He smiled as he spoke. He had as keen a nose for pain as a dog has for deer, and he knew that Manawyddan hated to be reminded that he was Bran's heir, should Branwen fail to have issue.

"I have always refused to hold either land or lordship," Manawyddan said quietly. "That you and all men know. Let the boy be."

"Now I call that unfair," said Evnissyen. "He answered me shortly just now, when I asked him a simple question, and yet I have been taking his part."

"In your own way," said Manawyddan, then bit his

lip. To answer Evnissyen was always unwise; it gave him an excuse to speak again. Yet the place that is always being pricked grows sore.

Manawyddan knew the dangers of Evnissyen's endless pricking. Big, good-natured Bran would have wanted to pull down the moon if his baby had cried for it, and though Caradoc, left to himself, would no more have dreamed of crying for kingship than of crying for the moon, Evnissyen was forever reminding him of what otherwise the lad would have taken for granted. Making him feel deprived of something, and making sure that he could not forget that deprivation.

Evnissyen shrugged now and said, "Well, whatever I do is always wrong. I should be used to your thinking that, you sons of Llyr. You are both better than I; all my brothers are better than I. I have always had the pleasure of knowing that everybody thought that. And maybe it is true. For if ever I refused lands and lordship, it would be because those offered me were not big enough. Because I hoped to get more by waiting; by being good, so very ͺood that presently people would thrust what I wanted upon me as a duty."

Manawyddan looked straight at him with the sea-gray, sea-deep eyes of Llyr. "It is to be hoped that such cunning would take more baseness than is on you, son of my mother, as it would take more than is on me."

Bran said disapprovingly, "That was a big long mouthful of nothing, brother Evnissyen."

He had turned from the cliff drop and the mist, and was watching them, but Manawyddan wished that he had not. Here was mist more blinding to a man.

Evnissyen flushed. "Then you love Caradoc less than you claim to, brother. Why should not the boy have all that kings' sons in the Eastern World already have? —what many think that some day all kings' sons will have! With Manawyddan's help, that surely such an unselfish man should hurry to give, you could change the laws. Make Caradoc king after you."

Manawyddan said, "You have heard my answer to that over and over—you and Bran both. For Bran to do that would be to declare himself no rightful king. Then Caswallon could say justly, 'Why should Caradoc follow Bran, when I could not follow Beli?' All the Island of the Mighty might become chaos, with sons and nephews fighting one another for inheritance."

Bran sighed. "That is true—and yet hard to take. For some day the change will come."

"Then why not now?" demanded Evnissyen. "In time for Caradoc. I know you love peace, but if trouble must come, why not get it over with?"

"Because in time to come that trouble may be less," said Manawyddan. "By then so many people may want the change or at least be ready to accept it that it may come without turmoil and strife."

Then he bit his lip again and thought, *I should have let Bran answer him.*

Evnissyen grinned again. "Well, you cannot be blamed for wanting things to stay as they are, Manawyddan. You are the man who would lose most by the change."

Bran opened his mouth to speak, then closed it. Silence fell; silence that seemed to stretch and knit and tighten, like cords around living flesh.

Evnissyen could have hugged himself. He lay down and threw one arm over his face to hide the joy in it. *Bran will not believe anything that I have said, but it will bother him. And it will bother Manawyddan, and seeing that will make Bran wonder. If he ever should believe it—! He shivered with delight.

He did not know why he wanted to set his brothers at odds; he did not hate them much more than he did other men. But his belief that he had been wronged and insulted all his life was by now so deep-rooted that he never bothered to think who had wronged him or how, only revenged himself constantly upon all. This was the quality of Evnissyen; he held his own dignity and that of any other person with whom he might briefly identify himself (he never exactly liked anybody) to be as delicate as eggshell. He could think of a thousand ways in which that precious fragility could be hurt; he hunted such hurts with an eye keener than a hawk's. He could convince a man whose elbow had been jostled in a crowd that that jostle had been long premeditated and deliberate, and he could make that man burn to avenge the malicious outrage. People said that he could make trouble between a man and a woman about to lie together, between the woman's own two breasts. Certainly trifle-twisting and troublemaking were his gifts. And he had made trouble now.

Manawyddan sat and thought, *My brother cannot think that I want his place. Yet he heard what Evnissyen said; he sat there and said nothing* . . .

Bran wondered uneasily whether he should have rebuked Evnissyen again. Yet to keep rebuking such twaddle was to seem to take it seriously. Manawyddan knew Evnissyen as well as he did. Why was he getting so sensitive about what the boy said? And why should he be so set against Caradoc's getting the kingship? Caradoc . . . Caradoc . . . The lad would make so fine a king.

What he thought was clouded by what he felt and wanted, and the poison of Evnissyen worked on.

Caradoc too was silent. Like nervous birds his eyes flew back and forth between his father and his uncle, wary yet yearning. If those two willed it, he could be a king . . .

Manawyddan caught those glances. The silence began to weave itself a tongue, and that tongue accused him. He rose.

"Have I your leave to go, Lord?"

Bran stiffened. "Why should you wish to go, brother?"

"It seems to me best, Lord."

Bran looked down; thought wearily, *Why should I always have to be telling him how honorable he is? I have said nothing against his honor.*

His hesitation lasted a little too long. It pierced Manawyddan like a spear. He said in a low voice, "I think it is the King's will that I should go."

Bran said with a rumble like a bear's growl deep in his great throat, "Why should I wish that, Manawyddan?"

Manawyddan said with a coldness that was like an icy crust over boiling heat, "That is for you to tell me, Lord. But I think that you will not—to my face. For you only play with it in the darkness inside your head. You know well that it is not worthy of the light."

Then Bran's voice leapt forth like the roar of a lion. "I dare say whatever I think, brother. Why do you think that I am thinking evil about you—unless you have first got that evil formed in your own heart?"

Manawyddan's face went death-white. "Name that evil, King."

Silence again; silence that tightened around necks like a noose. Bran looked at Manawyddan, and Manawyddan looked at Bran. Evnissyen leaned forward, his face eager as fire.

The silence dragged at Bran's mouth and tongue like wild horses. His mouth opened; he was afraid of what might come out of it. He wanted to shut it, but could not. The muscles of his throat moved. Sound whistled between his teeth and died there.

Somebody had laughed.

Laughter, cool and sweet as the bubbling of a spring, it shattered that grim silence as gently as though melting it. And the fierce suspicions of Evnissyen's breeding and begetting slunk away like dogs, their tails between their legs.

"What is all this about?" Nissyen, the son of Penardim, looked at his elder brothers. "Why are you two making the air red around you? Tell me."

But of a sudden they both knew that there was nothing to tell Nissyen. They felt him, as if he had been cool air in a heated place; a cool clean wind, blowing through their hearts as well as their lungs. Bran himself laughed, as if at some vast and incredible joke.

"Nothing at all, Nissyen, nothing at all. Manawyddan here is insulted because he thinks I have got it into my head that he wants to be king after me. A long reign he would be looking forward to, since I am only two winters older than he is, and very healthy."

He beamed down upon his younger brothers, tolerant, enlightening, jovial. "I would be the world's biggest fool to keep a notion like that in my head long," he said.

"As big a fool as I would be to think you could," said Manawyddan, and put out his hand. Bran took it, and they both laughed. Nissyen laughed with them.

"You would be a pair of fools," he said.

Evnissyen sprang to his feet, savage as a hungry dog whose bone has been snatched away. "It is I that had better go away," he said. "I am not wanted here. I never am."

Bran looked at him levelly. "It is not you that are not wanted, boy. It is the kind of thing you start."

But Evnissyen was already gone, his red cloak whirling round him like a flame hissing over dry leaves.

"He is hurt." Nissyen looked after his twin, and in his eyes was pity. "He thinks always that you two hold it against him because he is Eurosswydd's son. Always, since we were little, whenever anyone has been angry with him he has thought that that was the reason—not anything that he himself has done."

"Among the Old Tribes it never has mattered who a man's father was," said Bran. "And whoever his mother was it always has been held that he himself deserved good treatment because he was here at all. But if Evnissyen does not watch out, some day it may matter who he himself is."

"So far he has done nothing but what others let him do," said Nissyen. That was the quality of Nissyen; he always told the truth.

Bran did not answer that. He sighed again and sat down beside Manawyddan. Nissyen sat down near them. Caradoc went back to playing with his ball. There was quiet again upon the Rock of Harlech, and peace settled down like a nesting bird. That too was the quality of Nissyen; he made peace.

Bran looked out to sea again. The mists had lifted, and in that clearness and from that great height, he seemed to be looking out into unearthly space. Sea and sky were before him, and sky and sea, and far away the two seemed to meet, vast blueness clasping vast blueness, in an embrace that looked like the world's end. In earlier times, when boats were new, and a thought but recently shaped into wood by the hands of men, folk had believed that blue wall solid. The boldest had tried to sail out to it, to see what it looked like near at hand. But when always it had recoiled before them, a space farther off for every space that they advanced, they had concluded that it was magical, a druid work set up to veil Other World secrets from the eyes of men.

Bran watched the delicate shining mystery of that wall until the sun came down to cleave it, filling the sky with blood and spilling gold upon the darkening sea.

Then he saw speckles cross that flaming disc. Speckles that grew and swelled into strange shapes, like huge ants crawling across the face of the dying sun. Swiftly they grew—speeding forward, out of Illusion, into the world of men.

They became birds, great birds with white wings spread, darting toward the land, their prey.

Bran raised his hand. "Ships are coming—and coming fast."

There was a sudden stir around him. All men were on their feet, all eyes looking where he looked. Excitement the many-fingered, that has hands enough to grasp all near her, had them by the throats. One or two strange ships might be either pirate or peaceful traders, but never before had so many ships come toward the Island of the Mighty save as invaders.

Bran said, "Do you go down and lead men out to meet them, Manawyddan. But go as a herald; find out whether they come in peace."

Some men stared as if they thought him mad, but in the faces of others hope dawned. The King was not sure that the strangers came as foes.

Manawyddan signed to men who took spears and shields and followed him. Round all their hearts the subtle many-fingers tightened—so swift and sure and silent was that advance across the reddened sunset sea, with the wind behind it, the wind upon which ride Other World folk and the disembodied dead.

On the shore below, men were milling around, rushing to arm themselves. With shouts they greeted the son of Llyr, thinking he had come to lead them. Manawyddan smiled and raised his hand palm outward, commanding peace.

"Have your spears ready, men, but do not cast them until I give the word."

Then all were silent, looking out to sea.

Nearer the strange ships came, and nearer. Never had the men of the Island of the Mighty seen ships more splendid. The stranger-vessels glowed and bloomed with many-colored banners of rich stuffs, with men in many-colored clothes and shining arms. In the red light their bronze breastplates and spearheads shone like fire, brighter than gold.

One ship sailed ahead of the others, and as they looked, men lifted up a great shield above its side, pointing outward, in token of peace. Manawyddan's heart lightened when he saw that, for the sons of Llyr did not love war; but he did not sign to his men to lower their spears. There might be treachery.

Behind the shield a tall man appeared, scarlet-cloaked. The sharper-eyed saw that he wore no helm; the sun caught in his bright hair and in the brighter circlet that banded it. A king's crown.

When the ships came close beneath the Rock of Harlech, he raised his arms and from his throat and from the throats of all his men a mighty shout pealed across the waters.

"Greeting! Greeting to Bran the Blessed, Lord of the Island of the Mighty!"

From his place high above, Bran heard them. He leaned forward, and his own great voice boomed out across the waters. "The Gods give you good, strange men! A welcome is with you here. Whose ships are these, and who is your chief?"

His voice seemed to come from the sky above them, and the strangers started and stared. They had taken Manawyddan's tall, tree-straight figure waiting on the shore for the mightier son of Llyr. Then a herald rose and said, "Matholuch the High-King of Ireland is here. These are his ships, Lord, and we are his men."

"Why is he here?" said Bran. "Is he coming ashore?"

"He is not," said the herald, "unless he gets what he wants. He has come to ask a boon of you, Lord."

"Well," said Bran, "what is it?" He made no promises; granting an unnamed boon could be a riskier business than buying a pig in a poke, as Pwyll Prince of Dyved had learned at his wedding feast, when Gwawll tricked him, that dangerous suppliant out of Faery.

"It is Branwen of the White Breast, Branwen the daughter of Llyr. Let her go with him and be his wife, Lord, that you and he may be as brothers, and the two Islands of the Mighty be leagued, and both grow greater."

Then indeed silence fell. Men stood and stared, too thunderstruck to be angry. Never had a woman of the Old Tribes left her kin and her island save as the victim of fraud or force. Such a thing was unheard of, incredible; and the woman so asked for was Branwen, their noblest lady, the mother of the kings that were to come.

Bran broke that silence; he rubbed his chin. "Well," said he, "that is a boon. I am no king of the Eastern World to give my sister away like a cow. But let your king come ashore and feast with us; let the girl get a look at him, and we will talk about it."

On the shore below, men stared and stared again, as though they could not believe their ears. But the herald smiled, and the tall man with the crown whispered in his ear.

"Lord, King Matholuch thanks you. He will gladly come ashore."

Near Manawyddan one man plucked up heart enough to slap his thigh and mutter, "Well, when that outlander comes ashore he will get what he has asked for. And it will not be Branwen!"

Another laughed. "Bran is clever! He has to get the fellow ashore to be able to punish him."

A man of the New Tribes said thoughtfully, "At least he is coming ashore without knowing whether he will get her or not. Bran has made him back down."

Manawyddan said nothing; he stood like a tree, like a rock. He knew better than to hope that there was guile in Bran's offer; he knew his brother. For the first time in his life fear froze him; icy fear. *Will he send the girl away with strangers? So far away that we can know what happens to her only by hearsay? Rob her of her home, and her children of their heritage? Can he dote on Caradoc enough to do that?*

The Irishmen came ashore; proud, fine men clustering around their king. He was tall and comely, Matholuch; indeed, no man with any blemish might be High-King in Tara. His silky hair and beard were almost red, but in the dying sunlight they shone with a glitter that was golden. His keen eyes were almost blue, yet too pale for blueness; no young comely woman ever looked into them without dreaming of being the sunrise that would warm them.

On the shore he gave Manawyddan the kiss of peace and greeting, and on the Rock, Bran gave it to him. Then Branwen came, the daughter of Llyr. Bran had sent for her and her maidens.

She was beautiful, the sister of Bran the Blessed. Her hair was like the wings of blackbirds, and her breast was like the breast of a white dove, soft and warm and sweet, the loveliest of all flesh in the world. Matholuch's whole face shone when he saw her.

"By the sun and by the moon, and all the elements, Lady, you are worth a journey to the world's end!

Sorrow is on me for all the nights I have slept without you!"

Her face crimsoned, even her white breast. She said, "Greeting, and joy be with you, Matholuch of the Irish."

He laughed a great laugh. "Indeed it will be, Lady, if you will it." He took the mead cup that she offered, his great hand brown on her white arm. And the shadows that were lengthening over Harlech grew blacker.

Like a great cloak darkness fell. Fires gleamed; beasts were slain and turned on spits above those fires. The men of the two islands sat and ate, and the women of the Island of the Mighty ate with them.

Branwen sat across from Matholuch, and her eyes were filled with the beauty and brawn of him. Her heart sang, *Here is my man, my first man and my last, the one for whom I have always waited.* Yet some space deep within her was cold with dread. To leave her home and her people forever—the girls she had played with and grown up with, her kin, her brothers, Bran and Manawyddan, Nissyen and Caradoc, even Evnissyen—how could she do it? Yet if she did not, if she watched this man sail away, would not all things that were left behind be cold and empty and hollow?

If she could have gone back to that morning, to the time when she had never seen him, how gladly, how happily, she would have fled there! But now, whatever she did, everything must be changed; pain and rending loss were inescapable.

And yet—and yet—did she truly wish that she had never seen him? Missed the sight and sound and warm nearness of him, the knowledge that such a man existed?

She could not go with him! she could not! Yet . . .

Her eyes begged him to make her go, yet not to make

her. To do the impossible, and take the pain out of sorrow.

With green, hungry cat's eyes he watched her; the clean, swan lines of her head and throat that curved down into the warmer, richer beauty of her breast. He burned to lay his head and hands there, on that warm white sweetness that was a nest for love. Yet he never forgot what else that lovely body was: a strategic treasury, the shaping place, the gateway into this world of kings to come. Of the lords of this island that was greater than his own ...

Not until near dawn were the sons of Llyr alone together. Then, when the fires had burned to embers and all other men had gone to rest, when the moon had set and the earth lay lightless and forsaken, they talked together.

"Well," said Bran, "it is plain that Branwen likes him. What have you to say, brother?"

"I do not like it," said Manawyddan. "No king in the Western World ever before has sent his sister away with an outlander."

"You give the best of all reasons for doing it," said Bran. "That word 'outlander.' The Old Tribes dwell in Ireland, as in our own isle. The New Tribes followed them there, as here. We are of one blood; or of the same bloods. Yet a little strip of sea has built such a wall between us that men of each island call those of the other 'outlanders,' and make of that name a suspicion and a stink."

"That would be as wrong if our bloods were different, brother."

"True. It is not honorable or a hero's deed to kill a man because he does not live where you live, or in some other way is different from you. But all our young men, Matholuch's and ours alike, think it is; by stealth these young hotheads raid each other's shores and slay and steal and burn. It is no use to talk about who did that first, or who does it oftenest. The thing to do is to stop it."

Manawyddan said, "I am not one to hold any man's race against him, Bran; you know that. But this man Matholuch is a stranger to us. And he springs from the New Tribes, whose ways are not our ways."

"He seems well-bred and well-favoured. All that a man should be, brother."

"Maybe. But I wish I could see him with his beard off. Many a face that is good at the top is poor at the bottom. All we know about his jaw is that he can eat with it."

"A needful accomplishment." Bran grinned.

"A father of kings needs more. Also, hate of outlanders will not die overnight. If Branwen's boy is born in Ireland his seat will not be easy when he comes here to rule."

For a breath's space Bran was silent. Then he said, "A king's seat is never easy."

"And Branwen herself, brother? The storm in her blood may drive her to Ireland, but there she will be what the man is here—an outlander. If troubles rise between them—and what is so chancy as this hot, all-creating, much-destroying love between man and woman?—she will be alone. All there will be his friends, not hers. And in Ireland the New Tribes have won the mastery; they who think that man should be master over woman."

"Matholuch would never dare to offer her harm or insult," said Bran. "Too many traders pass between the isles; it would soon reach our ears. Also, why should any man wish to hurt such as she? Branwen is lovable as well as lovely."

"Many women have been both, brother, yet woe has come to them."

"To come home again will always be in her choice," said Bran. "She is a woman of the Kings! No man dare lay bonds upon her. Beli made peace in this island, brother. If I could make it between the two islands . . ."

With the part of him that loved all men and all women Bran looked upon that picture and saw that it was good. If, deep in the darkest, unacknowledged places within him something whispered, *Branwen's son will be born far away. He will be a stranger in the Island of the Mighty, when Caradoc is known and loved,* he did not tell himself that he heard.

Manawyddan sighed. "I see how you will speak in council, brother, before the chiefs. As you know well how I would like to speak. But I will not go against you there. I never have."

He thought, *Friendship between peoples, the death of old hates—with what fine clothes you have covered the nakedness of your desire. You hide your true purpose from yourself, but it is there.*

2

The Insult

In the Council of the Chiefs that Marriage was agreed upon, the first marriage ever made for reasons of state-craft in the Island of the Mighty. Bran the Blessed and his sister wished it, and his brothers Manawyddan and Nissyen said nothing against it. His brother Evnissyen was not there to say anything. Since that day when he had failed to estrange his elder brothers upon the Rock of Harlech no man had seen his face.

The *Mabinogi* says that it was settled that Branwen should first admit Matholuch to her bed at Aberffraw. So Bran marched there with all his men, and Matholuch sailed there with all his ships. Too many were those wedding guests to have been got into any house. They ate and slept in tents and around campfires. At night the stars, watching those many bright fires upon the once dark earth, must have wondered and searched the sky for a gap in the constellations, shivering lest they too should fall.

Beside one fire sat the sons of Llyr, and across from

them sat Branwen the daughter of Llyr beside Matholuch, and the hands of the two lovers were forever
touching, and their eyes stealing long deep looks.
Manawyddan watched them and thought, *It is like
wine, this thing between them. I hope that it will last.
But I do not like it, this plan for two people to sleep
together for the good of two islands. Desire will not
always come when it is called. A dreary road to set
winding through the ages—the loveless beds of weariness, and the children begotten without joy. Well, maybe it is as well for the Great Going-Forward that Bran
is king, not I. I am not one to open up new roads.*

He looked again at Branwen, at her sweet, flushed
face and her eyes that saw only the Irishman, and he
prayed to the World-Fashioners by the name he knew
Them by: *"O Mothers, who made the earth, make my
sister's road as good as you can!"*

That night Matholuch slept in the arms of Branwen
the white-breasted, the daughter of Llyr.

Day came again and night, and after them day and
night again, the black and the gold shuttling back and
forth as they will till the world ends. For the marriage
between light and darkness seems likely to have been
the first ever made, as it will certainly be the last,
when that energy which has been perverted into darkness is at last purified and drawn back into that Breast
of Divine Fire from which it came.

Branwen and Matholuch were happy. Day after day
the Irish King hunted and feasted with the men of the
Island of the Mighty, and night after night he lay
down beside his wife, and for them there was no sunset
and no darkness, only their own fire that rose up and
walled them in and left them alone to love each other.

His men hunted and feasted too, and found the
women of the Island of the Mighty most hospitable,

and his horses grazed all the way from Aberffraw to the sea. The Irish men and the Irish horses lived on the fat of the British land, and one may wonder which frisked the more.

Evnissyen came upon the horses on his way home. What happened makes it certain that he did not come upon many Irishmen. Likely there was only one Irishman, with the horses, and he old.

Evnissyen had been in the hills, sleeping upon hard ground, and eating what game he could catch, hearing no human voices, only the cold winds that blew over him and paid no heed to him. Such impersonal foes, unlike an angry person to whom one hates to yield, do not challenge the proud *I* and are often very cooling. Evnissyen was ready now to forgive his brothers; indeed, he felt almost friendly toward them.

He wanted to get home, but when he saw the horses he stopped to look at them, and no wonder, for they were well worth looking at. From hock to forelock they were perfect, from mane to tail they were all swift, shining beauty. Their eyes and their sleek coats shone like stars. Ireland has bred many fine horses, but none anywhere have ever outshone these.

"Here are fine beasts," said Evnissyen. "Whose are they?"

"Who is your honor himself?" said the Irishman, grinning. He thought that this was Nissyen, being playful. The two sons of Eurosswydd were as alike outside as they were unlike inside, dark slender youths with great beauty in their faces, like Penardim their mother.

Evnissyen did not grin back. He felt that he was being made fun of, and his ever tender dignity promptly puffed up again and became as prickly as a porcupine.

"I am brother to the High-King of the Island of the Mighty, fellow. To Bran the Blessed himself. I am

Evnissyen, son of Penardim. So keep a civil tongue in your head, oaf."

That wiped out the Irishman's grin. "If you are a brother of King Bran," he said, "I take it that it is not because of you that he is called the Blessed. But if so, these horses are your kinsman's horses, for they belong to Matholuch, High-King of Ireland, and your sister Branwen's man."

Evnissyen went as red as fire and then white as death. "Is it so they have dared to deal with a girl like Branwen—giving her to a dog of an outlander? My own sister too, and my counsel unasked? My brothers could have put no greater shame on me than this."

It seemed to him that Bran and Manawyddan had arranged this marriage on purpose to punish him, to show him and all the Island of the Mighty of how little account he was in their counsels or in any great matter, the least of the sons of Penardim. They had not waited for him, they had jumped at the chance to settle this unheard of great business without him!

His hands shot out and grasped the old man's throat. "By the Gods your people swear by! Is this shame true?"

"It is true, and no shame," said the old man sturdily. Evnissyen's sword went through his belly before he could say more. He fell, and the son of Eurosswydd stood and watched him die, glad of every groan. Then he rushed upon the horses and cut their ears off. He cut off their lips, and left their bare teeth with the blood running down them, gumless. He cut off their silky tails. He hacked away their eyelids. He did them every hurt he could, short of killing them, and all the while their screams were music in his ears. In his own mind he was cutting this off Bran, and that off Manawyddan, and several things off the unknown Matholuch. For once in his nervous, self-harried life he was happy, for if his revenge was incomplete and in part dream, he yet was spoiling complete beauty, and there is a kind of miracle in being able to undo such a miracle as that.

When he had done all the things he could think of to the horses, he went away. On the road he met another Irishman and stopped him.

"Tell your outland High-King," he said, "that he had better go look at his horses, for they were never so well worth looking at before. Also it is a pity to leave such fine beasts unguarded, and the man who was minding them is in no shape to do it now.

"Tell him too that this message comes from Evnissyen, brother to Bran the High-King, him that rules over by far the greatest of the Isles of the Mighty."

Laughing, he went upon his way, that no longer led home.

But the Irishmen were not laughing when they came to their King. Their faces were as red as blood, and their hands were knotted fists.

"Lord," they said, "you have been disgraced and insulted as no king in Erin ever was before you."

Matholuch stared. "How?"

"Lord, the horses have been cut and hacked about, castrated and left to their blind screaming. The cruelty of it passes belief. And Evnissyen, your lady's own brother, himself boasted of it to us. This must be what these other-island men have been planning from the beginning, while they slobbered over you and made-believe to be your friends."

Matholuch sat as stiff as a dead man, staring from crimson face to crimson face. He felt hollow, as if his vitals had been knocked out of him. He wanted time, time to think, but there was no time. All those red, staring eyes beat him like whips.

He tried, once, to use reason. Himself, he would have liked to wait for explanations; he was a temperate man. He licked his lips and said weakly, "It is a wonder to me why, if they meant to insult me, they let me sleep with so noble a lady, the darling of all her kin."

The hard red stares did not soften. "Lord, it does not matter what kind of a wonder it is. It is so. And since there are not enough of us here to fight them, there is nothing for you to do but to go home."

He saw that if he did not go they would despise him. He said heavily, "Let us be going then."

A white-faced girl brought news of that going to Branwen the Queen. At first Branwen laughed. The tale seemed madness, one of those ugly frightening webs that imps weave, out of the sleep-relaxed and un-guarded brains of men. But the day was plain and sane around her. The encircling soberness of reality pressed the tale upon her, something that must be dis-proved and thrust back into the land of dreams.

She went outside. She looked toward the road on the other side of her pavilion, the road that led down toward the sea and the Irish ships. She saw the Irish there, marching away, Matholuch at their head, tall and straight in his scarlet cloak. His face had the curious, carved look that all faces seen in profile have. Feelingless, masklike, image-like. He was going past her, they were all going past her, like stones set rolling by an avalanche. Men no longer, only moving images. It was a kind of death.

"Matholuch!" She tried to scream his name, but a sudden growth in her throat choked her. She tried to run after him, but her feet had grown roots that shot down into the earth and held her.

She wanted to throw her arms around him, and turn

him back from image to man again. *Yet what if she
should touch him, and he should not come alive?*

He was more a stranger now than on that first
day. An image going away from her with the images
of his men. No cry of hers could reach him, or that
silent company, any more than if they had been dead
men going down through the Pass of the Dog's Mouth,
down into the misty fields of Arawn, Lord of the
Underworld.

It was surely her death. For her man, her lover,
wanted to go.

Bran and Manawyddan sat in council in the royal
camp of Harlech. Evening had come, but not the
peace of evening. The sky blazed with terrifying color,
blood-red and fire-gold.

Their councilors sat with them, but they talked
low. Branwen was in the pavilion behind them, and
the sons of Llyr hoped that she was safe in the arms of
sleep, that gentle sister of death. She had not wept,
but her silence had been worse than weeping, heavy
and dumb as the pain within her.

Bran had sent messengers after Matholuch. They
had spoken with him aboard his ship, that his men
were loading. They had said, "Lord, this business was
not willed by our King or his councilors. The shame
on Bran the Blessed is worse than it is on you. It is
unblessed he has been this day."

"That is what I think," said Matholuch. "His face
is more blackened than mine. But he cannot take back
the insult. He cannot undo the pain."

Bran's men made offers of atonement then, and
Matholuch looked around at his men. But he saw
only one face engraved on many faces, eyes bright and
jaws set rigid with pride in their own anger. And he
said, "Red was the wrong, and red must any atone-

ment be. And that kind I do not think your King will want to pay us, since the man who did the wrong is who he is."

The messengers brought these words back to Bran, who sat long in silence. Every man heard that silence; felt it, like a knife at his throat. For but one true atonement could be made to Matholuch.

Manawyddan spoke at last, and his voice was like the unsheathing of a sword. "Two things we must settle. What we are going to do about the Irishmen, and what we are going to do with Evnissyen."

"We could exile Evnissyen," Bran said drearily. "The Mothers know he has deserved it, and without sinning against the Ancient Harmonies we can offer Matholuch no greater face-price. Never among the Old Tribes has brother slain brother. Even among the New it is still accounted an evil deed. We cannot do it."

"If we exile him," said Manawyddan, "he will turn pirate and treat the people of Ireland's coast—and maybe of ours—as he did the horses."

Bran groaned. "Why could not one of those horses have kicked him in the head?"

"It did not. We were not fated to get peace so easily, brother."

Bran groaned again. "This is an ugly business. His killing the Irishman I can understand. He has always liked despising things; naturally, he would despise an outlander and see no great harm in killing one. But this business with the horses—I have never heard the like. No man can have acted like that since the world began. Does he know no pity?"

His great face looked as heavy as if all the gloom of night had gathered there.

"We were fools not to foresee trouble," said Manawyddan. "He did have a right to sit in the council that decided to let our sister go with Matholuch. And his dignity has always been a tender part of him."

"I would like well to use my hand on another tender part of him," Bran growled.

"That too is against the custom of the Old Tribes," said Manawyddan, "To beat our young. We might have taught Evnissyen cunning, but we never could have taught him fear stronger than his hates."

Bran said grimly, "Many men might live if he died now. The druids were right, brother. You remember? When Nissyen was born they looked at him and shook their heads in wonder. They said, 'How could such a child have come of such a deed?' But when Evnissyen followed him they shook their heads again and said, 'Never let this one grow into a man upon the Island of the Mighty.'"

"I remember well," said Manawyddan. "I still can hear our mother's weeping. Llyr stood against the druids for her sake, and Beli would not judge between his people and his kin. He sent messengers to Math the Ancient, who replied that every child was a destiny, and that this one would not have come here if the island had not earned him. So Evnissyen was kept and named."

"Evnissyen—'unlike Nissyen,'" said Bran. "Which the Mothers know he is." He sighed. "I do not see what we island folk had done to earn him."

"Our mother Penardim did a deed," said Manawyddan. "Eurosswydd did a worse. Deeds have been in the air ever since the New Tribes came, because change has been in the air. Change that seldom bears a single child, but mostly twins—good and evil. But because Evnissyen is unlike Nissyen, are we to make ourselves unlike Bran, unlike Manawyddan? The Ancient Harmonies are in your hands to guard, brother. They and, I hope, the shape of the world that is to be."

Bran looked off into the night, that was moonless; at the stars that seemed to watch him like a myriad bright eyes. Such eyes as might shine from dark colossal faces watching, with quiet, age-old wonder, the turmoil of earth.

He said finally, "There is nothing we can do about Evnissyen. You could not let light into him, not if you made a hole in him. But the Irishman is another matter. Go after him, brother, with Heveydd the Tall and what other men you choose to take, and tell him that though I cannot give him the head of my mother's son—as indeed I would like well to do—I will give him such a face-price as never was paid to any king before." He named that price over.

"It is more than he is worth," said Manawyddan.

"It is his due. Nor do we want bitterness between the two islands, and all his young men raiding our coasts. I could not hold our folk then. Besides, this business is breaking Branwen's heart."

Manawyddan stiffened. "Let it break here, not in Ireland. Matholuch is not good timber to build a peace with, brother. He has not been staunch to Branwen."

"He has not. I know it. Yet he is not such a one as Evnissyen. So long as nothing stirs him up he will do well. I have the peace of two islands to guard. Help me, brother." Manawyddan was silent awhile; then he said heavily, "Sooner would I give him our brother's head than our sister to take home with him, out of our sight. Yet I see that you cannot withhold her if she is still willing to go. But do you hunt Evnissyen down and keep him under guard. Else there is likely to be something else to stir our precious new kinsman up."

"There will not be, Lords." Tall Heveydd had heard, and had come forward. "The Lord Nissyen

has gone to look for his brother. Yesterday he bade
me tell you so, but so much has happened that I forgot."

Bran and Manawyddan exchanged a long look.

"Strange," Bran muttered, "how Nissyen always
knows! A pity that he did not find Evnissyen before
Evnissyen found the horses. But he will find him; that
is sure."

Manawyddan nodded. "Yes. You and I would
have had to set druids to looking into water and into
crystal to find out where Evnissyen is, but Nissyen's
feet will lead him to him of themselves. It is a queer
bond between those two."

"It is indeed." Bran grinned. "When they were little
and Evnissyen bit the nurses and kicked the dogs
and tore up whatever he could lay hands on, so that
Branwen herself had to be guarded from him in her
cradle, he never once lifted hand to Nissyen. If his
twin came up and looked at him he would stop
whatever evil he was doing, and then shriek with rage
and run. Does he love Nissyen, or does he hate him
most of all of us, I wonder? Well, that is one problem
settled. May you have as good luck with the other,
brother."

"I will do my best," said Manawyddan.

In the last hour before dawn, when quiet and blackness lay heavily upon all things as though the world
mourned for her own death, he came to the ships of
the Irishmen. He hailed them; by the light of their
guttering torches he saw how their eyes glittered, sheen
without color, peering at him watchfully from under
their helmets.

Their spokesman said, "Go back, British man. There
is nothing to talk about. Our King sleeps."

"Wake him," said Manawyddan. "Tell him that

Manawyddan, son of Llyr, is here. The brother of his own wife."

"I am here." Beyond the man who had spoken a tall figure loomed up, faceless. He stood out of reach of the torchlight, many others pressing about him.

Manawyddan peered toward him, strained his eyes, trying to make out that featureless patch of paler darkness that was his brother-in-law's face. Suddenly, startlingly, it came to him that he was seeing Matholuch as clearly as he ever had seen him. Was darkness much more veiling than shape and color, than the pride of him among his fighting men?

The son of Llyr gave his message. Matholuch said, "I will talk this over with my men."

Manawyddan and his men waited. The black of night gave way to a sickly colorlessness that made the earth look old and tired and misshapen. The east grew gray as an old woman's hair. A cold wind blew, and on it the shrill buzz of voices came to the envoys: "A great face-price . . . If we do not take it we must raid their coasts for vengeance . . . Then they may invade us . . . Likely that is what they are trying to get an excuse to do . . . If we refuse this we will get more trouble and maybe more shame, and never again such an honor-price."

The dawn reddened. Matholuch came to the ship's side and leaned over. He looked down at Manawyddan and smiled his old frank, friendly smile. In the red light his hair and beard shone almost red, with a glitter almost golden.

"Come up, brother," he said, "and clasp hands with me. Meat and drink shall be set before you and your men. Nobody in the world could refuse so fair a face-price. My men and I are agreed on that. And it is glad I will be to get back to Branwen, my wife."

3

The Peacemaking

At sunset Nissyen the son of Eurosswydd had come to a hill not far from Aberffraw. Trees and rocks were there, but no sign of man. Like a gashed and burning greatness the sky brooded above it; blood-red, as though from mighty wounds. The rocks and trees shone dully in that red glow, that was like the shadow and the soul of blood.

Nissyen saw an oak, and something that crouched within the shadow of that oak, so still that to any searcher less subtle it might have seemed part of that shadow. But Nissyen felt the red darkness that boiled round it, foul as fetid waters, fiercer than the burning sky.

"Evnissyen," he said. "Brother."

His twin jerked as if pierced by a dart; then averted his eyes as though sight of that calm face were intolerable.

"It would be you." His teeth showed in a snarl like a beast's. "Why can you never leave me alone?"

Nissyen said nothing. He sat down beside his brother; he did not look at him or away from him. His undemanding, undisturbed friendliness was like the tranquil power of earth herself, that is too big for any man to shatter, too strong and soft and fertile for any fire to burn.

It made Evnissyen feel empty and futile. He clutched, as with both hands, at the fury that was slipping from him. He tore at the earth and got fistfuls of grass, and so the satisfaction of hurting something a little.

"He sent you!" he raged. "Bran."

And the bulk of Bran, that he had always feared a little, loomed over his mind like a great cliff, like the huge ice masses of the far north, immensities that, if one set in motion, might crush and chill all things.

"Is he still so pleased with the trick he played upon me, our glorious brother? He that has not guts enough to do what he wants and make his own son king? He has not pith enough in his whole vast clumsy carcass to resent an insult or insult anybody—except me. Except me!" He howled as a wolf howls. "All my life he has despised me. All of them have, all of them have always hated me and tormented me and twisted everything I ever said or did. Because I am Eurosswydd's son, not Llyr's."

"I too am Eurosswydd's son," said Nissyen. "I have never felt that hate."

"No, you crawling bootlicker! You hound, always whining at the heels of the sons of Llyr! But *I* have I have had to bear it all my days, and I will have to bear it all my days." He snarled and writhed in his agony, and tore up more grass.

"Grass feels less than horses," said Nissyen.

Evnissyen sat up. He laughed and ground his teeth in that laughter. "This anyway I have done! I have frightened them—Llyr's fine sons! I so nearly had them at each other's throats—I would have but for you, you blighting pest—that I made them afraid. This time it was me they tried to get even with—me." His voice rose in triumph. "Not our father. *Me*. Evnissyen."

"They should not have done it," said Nissyen. "But they did not do it out of malice. They forgot you."

Silence then, crashing silence. The sons of Llyr never could have made Evnissyen believe that they had been forgetful, not spiteful, but Nissyen made him believe. That knowledge made him feel small, and there was nothing in the world that Evnissyen feared so much as smallness—the smallness of himself. He loved giving pain, and so making himself large in the consciousness of that which felt the pain. He could have borne pain with secret delight in the knowledge that his own doings had been important enough to produce this violence that he suffered under, this disturbance and exertion in another being. To the chilled and starving inward person punishment can give a bitter nourishment. And now Evnissyen's source of food had been snatched from him.

When he spoke again his voice was low. "I will teach them to forget me! I am not a safe person to forget. If our good brothers have not learned that by now, soon they will learn it. Eurosswydd made them remember. I am glad of that. Glad that our mother had to have him when she did not want him. He got as much done with her in one night as Llyr had in all the years before. Two of us, as there are two sons of Llyr. He was a man, our father! And Llyr had to remember every night thereafter, as long as he lived, that Eurosswydd had been everywhere he had been—" He laughed wolfishly. "Well, I will not be less than you, Father. I too will make them remember me. I have only begun."

Nissyen did not answer. Shadows were everywhere now, like dark, long-limbed invaders swinging down from the sky. Ever thicker, blacker, stronger—a host of them covering the earth.

Evnissyen said presently out of the darkness, "I could have been happy if they had not hated me." He moved restlessly, his hands still tugging at the grasses, but no longer uprooting them. He was tired; his fury was spent. For all his boastful words he had no idea what he could do next to make Bran and Manawyddan remember him. His beautiful upturned face was tragic, pure with the purity of pain, and so more than ever like its calm counterpart beside him.

"Do you suppose Bran will be able to make peace with that outland king, brother? I hope not—I hope not!"

If he cannot, I will still have done something. I will still have size.

"Bran will offer him a great face price," said Nissyen. "More than he could win in battle."

"He might get my head in battle. Maybe he hopes to get it anyway." Evnissyen laughed grimly, but uneasily too.

"You know Bran would never give him that, brother."

"Truly that is great goodness in him—the son of my own mother! I do not even know that it is so, but no doubt you do. You know many things, you creeping spy—too many! But you did not know enough to find me before I found the Irish. How you would have loved to save those horses from me!" He laughed spitefully.

"I should have indeed," said Nissyen. His voice was like the night-covered rocks around them; it had no color and no weakness and no passion.

"Dog!" Again Evnissyen's wolf howl rose. "Dog, unworthy of our begetter. If you had been my true brother, if you had stood beside me against the sons of Llyr . . ."

"I have always stood beside you. I stand against none."

This time Evnissyen made no answer. He hid his face and gave himself up to his sick hatred of all things. Nissyen lay beside him and thought, *I have given him a little light, and it is burning him worse than his own fire. Well, it is my business to bring light.*

Presently he rolled over and laid his hand on his twin's shoulder. "Get up, brother. Let us go up into the hills for awhile, both of us. Away from other men."

Obedient as a child Evnissyen rose, but he kept his eyes averted; they burned with unabated loathing.

Together they went up into the hills, and no man saw either of them again until the Irish had sailed for Ireland.

Bit by bit the sun let down her golden hair upon the earth. Through that brightening greenness Manawyddan and Matholuch marched back together. Tall Heveydd had gone ahead to warn Bran of their coming, and when they reached Aberffraw the feast spread there was as great as that which had been spread for the wedding. Bran sat waiting for them, and with him Branwen. Pale and still as a carved image she sat, deep circles round her great dark eyes. Ever since morning she had been thinking, *When he comes, will it be the same? Everything all right again, and I sure of him, my man? O Mothers, let it be the same!*

Yet could even They undo what once had been done?

Manawyddan and Matholuch came to Bran, and gave him the kiss of greeting. Then Matholuch came to Branwen. He took her in his arms and gave a great laugh—laughter, that needs no logic, is often more useful than words—and kissed her mouth, and rumpled her beautiful hair that had been smooth as black feathers.

"Well, girl," he said, "I missed you last night. Did you miss me?"

She laughed too and kissed him. But her eyes did not smile. They searched his as a tired swimmer's might search the horizon for land.

He sat down beside her, and ate. All ate, and soon talk buzzed as merrily as bees. Now that peace had been made and their mouths were full the Irishmen liked the British better, and because their mouths were full and the danger to their coasts was over, the British liked the Irish better. The two hosts liked each other.

Only where the Kings sat was there still a kind of silence, cold depths that the talk rippling over their surface could not warm. It may have had a quiet that came from Branwen; it certainly had an ugly red gloom that came from Matholuch.

For now that his men had forgotten the insult, he was remembering it. They, who had been honestly offended and outraged, could forgive. But they had dragged him after them. He, who should have been the head of the dog, had been its tail instead, and a well-wagged tail at that. He felt lessened. Both Branwen's silence and Bran's cheerful friendliness grated on him. Had his men been right at first? Was Bran laughing at him? At a little quarrel with a lesser king?

A lesser king . . . The darkness around him thickened.

Bran saw how white Branwen was, the depth of trouble in her still unsmiling eyes. He felt Manawyddan growing quieter and quieter beside him, saw the glitter of the sea growing in those sea-gray, sea-deep eyes. The eyes of Llyr their father.

Bran made a decision. He looked at Matholuch and said, "You are not as cheerful as you were, sister's man. If that is because you think the face-price less than you have a right to, you shall have any other goods of mine that you may ask for."

That was an offer as big as Bran, and for a breath's space it and his ox-big, guileless eyes washed Matholuch clean.

"Lord," the Irish King said, "that is a princely offer."

"It is meant to be, brother. I will add to the face-price; I will give you a rare gift. A cauldron that was not made upon this earth. This is its quality: if a man of yours were to be killed today," here he remembered sadly that Evnissyen had killed one of them yesterday, "you could throw him into it and he would jump out of it alive and whole, save that he would lack the power of speech. For it would not be himself that was in it, but some other thing in his body, something unable even to think in the tongues of earth. But he would fight like the demon he probably would be."

Red leapt into the face of Matholuch. His eyes shone.

"I give you thanks, Lord! That must be the greatest treasure in the Island of the Mighty. With it a man could conquer the world!"

"It is the best treasure a man could have," Bran said dryly, "to make invaders afraid to come against him. But a wise man would hate to use it. For those unearthly beings that can do nothing but fight might be worse to deal with, once his battles were won, than any earthly foe."

"I see." Matholuch's face fell. "Too great a risk would he take who tried to go forth and conquer with it. But it would make him safe from conquest. For at worst those Other World beings would walk the earth in flesh that once was of his own race. His people never would have the shame of bowing to outlanders."

Bran said still more dryly, "A hard choice. But you see what I meant you to see."

Night had come again; all the feasters went to their rest. Branwen and Matholuch went to their pavilion, his arm around her. So it had held her on other nights, cradling her, warming her like wine. But now, back again in that longed-for, magic-making circle, she still felt cold and lonely, like a lost woman wandering in the winter night.

They were in her pavilion now, and she heard him sending her women away. "Go and get some sleep now, girls. I will help your lady get her clothes off." Always before that laugh had thrilled her; it did not now.

She sat down on the bed; she felt tired, as a worn-out old woman is tired, for whom nothing has glow or sweetness any more. Her feelings had passed over her like years, slow and hard and aging years, and she had no longings left. Unless it was to be alone, not to go through a mockery of what had once been beautiful.

She felt his hands on her, undoing her dress, slipping down—somehow it offended her, as though he really were making love to an old woman, or to a corpse.

She said, "You did not want me so much last night."

He laughed again. "Did I not? Little you know about it, woman!" and pulled her close. He held her so tightly that she felt the reddish-gold hairs on his chest, the hard beating of his heart.

"Let us stop talking, sweet woman. Let us waste no more of the hours of this night!"

His arms held her fast; she could no more keep them out of her blood than she could have kept them off her body. Yet in them she could have wept because she was still shut out from him, still the wandering woman, peering through a lighted window at unreachable warmth and joy . . . Two Branwens; the body that was being comforted, and the woman who watched, alone with her inexorable knowledge, in the cold and the dark.

When he had possessed her and she still had not fully responded, he asked her what ailed her. "Nothing," she said, and her voice quavered on the word, and that shamed her; she was very young. Then, for the first time, she wept.

"Oh, how could you leave me without a word?"

He had no mind to quarrel with her; he wanted her and he wanted the Cauldron. The Island of the Mighty seemed a good place to him that night; pleasant and full of treasures. Besides, the cause of her distress flattered him. He held her tenderly and said the one thing that was left for him to say. "I was mad last night. I was shamed and grieved and enraged. I did not think."

That made him sound like a child carried away by his fury, and most women have tenderness for the hurts of a child. And though she did not want to she was still weeping, and he was fondling her to soothe her, though she still thought that she wanted him to go away.

"Branwen," he said, "Branwen." His voice was a lover's; the music that is at once delight and demand. His hands were stroking her breast, and they were warm. They brought a melting sweetness to every chilled hurt place within her.

"Matholuch!" she said. "Matholuch."

This time she was wholly his.

The Cauldron pleased the Irish. Before the feast was over, Bran's men had set it before the tents of the outlanders, huge and round and dully glinting, like a burnt-out, fallen star. It's new owners were full of wine and food and happiness, but they could not sleep for touching it and looking at it.

Yet all feared it a little. It seemed colder to the touch than it should be. Unearthliness was on it, the chill of black wastes beyond earth. Metal does not belong to our world alone; it may come to it from without, housed in meteors, those strange strays from the dark fields of space.

One man said, "I wonder if that British King was fooling us again." And he ran his hand along the side of the Cauldron gingerly, as if afraid it might resent his doubt and bite him. "Or if you really could kill a man and stew him in this, and him jump out as good as new except for not being able to talk."

"That last would be an improvement in some men I know," laughed a second. "Many a tongue has wagged off the head it was in."

"Indeed and indeed I would like well to see this Cauldron at work," said a third. He stared at it with wide, fascinated eyes.

"Until we do we cannot tell what it will do," said a fourth. "We have only this King Bran's word for it, and him an outlander, no Irishman. It would be a nice thing if, when we got it home and put a dead man in it, he only cooked."

"Before you can try it out you must have a dead man to put in it," said a fifth, "and nobody around here is dead."

They were silent awhile then. They were all eager to see the Cauldron work, but none of them wanted to be dead.

"We might draw lots," one hardy soul said at last.

But another promptly said no to that. "If the Cauldron did not work, then the King would be short a man."

They all discovered depth and greatness in their love for Matholuch. They said loyally, "That would never do. Here in the midst of his enemies. He needs every man he has."

"We might creep up on one of these outlanders and slit his throat and fetch him here," suggested one.

"That would not be honorable," said another.

"Nor safe," said yet another. "He would be missed in the morning, and we might be suspected. We might be caught killing him too, and then folk would say that we had broken the peace."

The first man sighed. "It is a pity not to be able to kill even one of them, after what they did to the horses. I helped rear those horses." He sighed harder. "Is there nobody we can kill at all?" he said.

"There is not," said the most cautious man, "but there is somebody we can dig up. Our comrade who was slain. Let us go and get him."

There was another brief silence. They all looked at one another doubtfully. "He has been dead a little while," said one. "He must be getting used to it."

"It happened only day before yesterday," said the man who wanted to dig him up. "He cannot have gone very far, and it is likely that he is still surprised and homesick."

They went and got him, and it took all of them to do it, though he had never been a big man. They shivered when they heard the wind moan as they carried him back through the quiet fields, for they thought his soul might be riding it, wondering angrily why old friends and kinsmen disturbed his rest. Death makes a stranger of a man; however easygoing he may have been in life, none can be sure how his temper will be when he is dead.

Gently and carefully they lowered him into the Cauldron. The moonlight shone down upon his still face, that was as blank as a doll's, yet full of awful mysterious wisdom, like the face of that Corpse-God who is said to have been the teacher of ancient poets. It looked familiar to none of them, though some there may have been his sons, or his sister's sons.

One said to him, "Brother, we are doing this for the honor and glory of Ireland. It is proud you should be to help us."

But then he sprang back sharply. That still face seemed so without interest, so unhearing.

They brought wood and set a fire and lit it. Little flames licked up toward the Cauldron. Men looked at one another, troubled.

"It must be hot in there," said one.

Another said, "He cannot feel it." Then, with a shudder, "At least not yet."

The flames rose higher. Quickly, as if some unseen thing reached down, eager to draw them upward. The Cauldron glowed red and baleful, like a fallen star that hated its prison, the earth. Smoke began to rise from it and, suddenly, a hissing sound like the voice of a mighty serpent.

The hair rose on the heads of the watchers. They all leapt backward. One man tried to giggle, "Have you never before heard a pot boil?" but in the midst of that giggle his teeth chattered. They were all shivering again, though the heat of the fire reached for them like hands.

The smoke rose higher, blotting out the moon.

Then, of a sudden, it quivered and vanished. The fire sputtered and went out, as if all power had been drawn out of it, into some Otherwhere. The moon shone again.

From within the Cauldron came a sound of movement, of something stirring there. A yell went up from the men closest to it, and they jumped back still farther.

The men behind them made room for them joyfully. All shrank, and most wanted to run, but could not. Their feet seemed glued there, and their eyes, that longed to look away, were glued to the Cauldron.

On the lip of the great vessel hands appeared. Fingers that looked unpleasantly long, unpleasantly eager. There was a scrabbling sound, and a body swung itself over the side, its long legs, its shaggy hair and beard half covering the setting moon.

Its eyes shone greenish, and the dead firelight seemed to glow on within them, evilly.

It came to the ground in one spring, and glanced about it, without recognition, into the faces of the Irish. Its nostrils worked, like a dog's, as if seeking a scent it could not find. Then, with an unhuman scream of rage, it leapt for the nearest Irishman.

Before he could move, its teeth had torn out his throat. Before the swords and the combined weight of all there brought it to earth, it had seized two more men and knocked their heads together, so that their skulls smashed like eggshells. Bran and Manawyddan came running from the British tents, and Matholuch came running out of Branwen's.

They heard what had happened. They looked down at what lay dead again, hacked by many blades, and Bran mopped his forehead.

"You see now, brother," he said to Matholuch, "what I warned you of."

"Truly," said Matholuch, his voice shaking, "I never would wish any man of mine a rebirth like that."

"Your man himself was never troubled," said Bran. "He was safe with Arawn in the Underworld. With him who has power to hold what he has taken."

Matholuch shuddered and said no more. He went back to Branwen, as if seeking shelter from the Unspeakable.

"I am glad he takes it like that," said Manawyddan, looking after him. "He will be careful with that Cauldron now. I remember my thankfulness when you got it from Llassar. And my heart sank like a stone today when you gave it away again. I never would have."

"I gave it to Branwen's man," Bran said simply. "To prove my friendship beyond all doubt, by giving him what could make his island safe from ours, the bigger one, forever. I did not think that too great a price to pay for our sister's happiness, and for the peace of two islands."

"Can any but they two buy their happiness," said Manawyddan, "she and Matholuch?" He looked off into the gray gloom of the fields and the heavens. "I think, too, that it takes more than gifts to buy peace, brother."

4

The Iron House

A second night they feasted, the men of Ireland and the men of the Island of the Mighty. And Matholuch said to Bran the Blessed, "Brother, where did you get that Cauldron?"

"From a man who came from your country, brother."

Matholuch started. "From an Irishman?"

"Where he first came from I do not know, but Llassar—the Flame—is the name he uses upon earth; and he is flamelike enough. He came here with his woman, Kymideu Kymeinvoll after they had escaped from the Iron House that your people heated red-hot around them. It is a wonder to me if you know nothing of that business, brother."

Matholuch smiled; a frank, open and soldierly smile. "I do indeed, for as High-King I ordered it heated red-hot around them. There seemed to be no other way for men born of women to defend themselves against those two, and their brood. I should have known that

60

Cauldron again; they were carrying it when I first set eyes on them."

"Tell us," said Bran.

"I will. One day I was hunting, and somehow I lost my way, and my comrades. I rode on and on, but whichever way I turned I seemed only to get deeper and deeper into the forest. Nothing but trees, trees everywhere; no beasts, no birds, not even a cricket singing. Only greenness and a great stillness, as if Earth Herself were holding Her breath down under the trees and grasses, waiting for Something that was to come. As if all life that had legs or wings had fled before that Something could come."

"Indeed," Branwen breathed, her lovely face flushed and her lovely eyes star-bright upon her husband, "you must have been riding into great danger."

Matholuch laughed and patted her hand. "No need to worry about that, girl, since I am here with you now. But then I did feel like a fish caught in a vast net, for the trees got so thick that I could not see the sky between their branches. Glad I was when toward evening, I saw the shimmer of water ahead, between the bushes. That meant a chance to drink, and an open place. But as I spurred toward the light a wind arose and screamed through the hidden sky. All the trees in the forest bent and shook and twisted. My horse and I rushed on, with branches snapping off and falling all around us. And then I heard a mighty, crashing splash, as of many trees falling into waters, and I knew that that shimmer must be a lake, and deep.

"We came out into the open, and I saw the surface of that lake churning as if there were a storm beneath it as well as above it. And in a breath's space I saw that that was so—that Something was heaving itself up from below."

He paused. Branwen caught her breath, and so did

all the women there. The faces of most men were tense. Only the sons of Llyr sat calmly, their sea-gray eyes fast upon the face of Matholuch.

He went on. "I saw a huge man's head and shoulders rise out of the lake. If you could call him man—his yellow hair was dripping, and his face was vast. Whiskers grew out of each nostril, and fringed each great thick roll of lip; fire-bright whiskers that looked as if they could burn up anything that touched them, and it was a pity they had not burned up the face. So I first saw Llassar, the Flame, and the sight of him was even more dreadful than fire, for which he is named.

"He rose out of the waters and waded toward shore, and I saw that he was carrying a cauldron on his back—this same, I suppose, that you gave me yesterday, Bran. But then I paid no heed to it. The waters were still churning, worse even than before he had come forth; and in a little while a woman's head rose out of them—if you could call her woman—and it was twice as high as his head, and twice as good to look away from. She waded after him like a farmwife shooing a hen. They came toward shore, and I saw her belly, and I hope I never see anything like that again!" He sighed, spat, and took a drink.

"What then?" Young Caradoc's face was eager.

"They saw me on the bank and called to me, 'Good day to you, Lord, and good be with you!' And I went down to meet them though I felt good might be nearer me if they were farther away from me. 'Well,' I said to the man, 'this is Ireland, and I am High-King of it, and why are you in it?'

"He said, 'This is the cause of our coming, Lord. In a month and a fortnight this woman with me will bear a son, and we must have some world for him to be born in. We ask your hospitality, Lord, for we are two strangers alone in your land.'

"Whoever or wherever they were I could not but feel sympathy for whatever people evidently had wanted that son of his born somewhere else. But to refuse such a plea would have been unkingly, so I took them home with me—I had no trouble in finding my way out of the forest once I had found them—and gave them a good farm. And the woman's womb, now that it was out of its own element, shaped flesh after the pattern of our world, for she gave birth to a stalwart, shapely youth. A sword, a spear, and a shield came out of her along with him, and that did surprise me, but I was glad not to have another monster on my hands, I was only one stout warrior to the good, and that sooner than could possibly have been expected.

"But next month she had another son, and the month after that another, and the month after that yet another. And the night that their youngest brother was born all four went out and stopped a party of nobles on the road to Tara. They stripped the men and took all their valuables, and they lay with all the women. Some of the women liked that and some did not, but none of the men liked it. They complained to me, loudly.

"I sent a man to complain to Llassar, but he found only Kymideu Kymeinvoll and the children at home, and he did not stay to deliver all his message, but went away quickly when Kymideu Kymeinvoll rose up and asked him what he meant by scolding her little ones so harshly."

"I begin to see," said Manawyddan, smiling grimly, "that you may have felt that your hospitality was ill rewarded."

"It was, brother. And next month Kymideu Kymeinvoll had another son, and that night all five went out and committed another and bigger outrage. Their mother said they were only playful and that we Irish could not take a joke, but Llassar seemed more understanding; he said he thought his boys might settle down if they had women of their own. So I gave them women, but they promptly got them with child and went on molesting my people the same as before. And every month there was another of them to help do it. At the year's end the chief men of Ireland came to me. 'Lord,' they said, 'you must choose between your realm and these children of Llassar the Killer—between his folk and your folk. If you keep on holding your hand over them we will outlaw you along with them, for we cannot stand them any longer. They must die.' "

" 'They may be hard to kill,' said I, 'for their father and mother may object.'

" 'The Old Ones must die too,' said they, 'them above all; for how can we ever hope for peace in the land while those two keep at it? No decent woman's insides could shape swords and shields. It is too tough that woman's insides are,' said they.

"So I sent men to slay the strangers by night, but Kymideu Kymeinvoll woke and killed twice as many of them as her man and boys did. I saw that I might lose a whole army that way, so I called a council of all Ireland. But while we were debating she had twins, and when we heard that we did not feel any better.

"Then a druid said, 'The great stone that fell from the sky last year has become metal; the metal that the Eastern world calls Iron. Iron is harder than bronze itself, that we make our swords from; none can break through it. Hollow a hall out of that stone, and it will hold even the Children of Llassar. Great was the toil, but we did it; then we made peace with the Llassar folk and bade them to a feast there, and we made them drunk. Then we slipped out and piled up charcoal, and built a great ring of fires round the Iron House."

"I know that part of the tale," said Bran shortly.

"It was a sight to see, brother. Every smith in Ireland helped, and every man that owned hammer and tongs. Flames roared like beasts, they shot up as if to eat the stars out of the sky. Soon would the heat within have grown unbearable to common flesh, to the children of men. And at last we heard a scream, as though a man's hand or arm, or some other part of him, had touched a red-hot wall. Some of us laughed then, for they had done many wrongs, they who were roasting in that oven."

Branwen was telling herself, *He had to do it. There was no other way.* But she was unhappy; when Matholuch paused for effect she said, "Did none of them get out?"

"Not then, Lady. The smiths blew upon the fires with bellows to make them yet hotter, and the people fetched yet more fuel. They danced round that ring of flame shouting and jeering at those within. But never another sound came from the Iron House. Until in the last hour of the second night, when those walls that had been red-hot glowed white as death, there came a great crash as the iron-plated doors burst outward. There the roaring walls of fire were thickest, but Llassar the Flame charged through them, and after him tramped Kymideu Kymeinvoll, her huge shadow dwarfing even his. Their children followed, but they were not so tall, and the flames blinded them. We spitted them like chickens, we thrust them back into the fire, though their giant parents fought hard to save them. Those two brushed aside our spears like pins, they thrust their long arms full-length into the flames. But in the end they had to flee, with only their Cauldron, whose power we did not know—good luck it was for us that they did not manage to fish out any of their boys' corpses to put into it! Where they went we never knew, nor did we care, since they went out of Ireland. I suppose they waded across to you, Lord?" He looked questioningly at Bran. "Through the Sinking Lands?"

"They did," said Bran, "and people here were not glad to see them coming. Many chiefs were for killing or driving them out. But I knew that that would cost many lives, also that, since they were here on earth, they had a right to live somewhere. So I made a bargain with them. They gave me the Cauldron, whose power they fear, and agreed to distribute their sons, as fast as they were born, among different towns and parts of the Island of the Mighty."

"You mean they are still here? That you have found no way to kill them?" Matholuch's jaw dropped. "How could you dare to give away the Cauldron?"

Bran laughed his great, deep, jovial laugh. Never was any sound on earth at once as mighty and as mellow, as thunderous yet serene, as the laugh of Bran. "We do not need it. We have eaten up that people and digested it."

"We did not have to cook it in an Iron House either." Disgust showed plain on Caradoc's young face.

For once Bran frowned at Caradoc; he did not consider that speech tactful. "Be still, lad. That savage brood is vast, Matholuch, but there is not much of it in any one place, nor does it know itself and hold together. But its people always prosper, and every town they live in they strengthen with the best of men and arms."

"You trust them?"

"Yes. I am not saying I am glad they came. That warlike stock, working within us, may yet change our race. But already we have changed them; they are part of us, of a large and peaceful people. Had I driven them on, they might have come upon some lesser land, and eaten up its folk."

"They may yet eat you up. Kymideu Kymeinvoll bears sons fast, brother."

This time Manawyddan laughed. "Not so fast now. In a whole year she has not borne a single warrior, yet you say that when your people got afraid and plotted her death she bore twins. Like breeds like, be it thought or flesh, and fear is wine to fury."

Bran said, "She did bear one more pair of twins, the first night after she came ashore here—the only children I have let her keep so far. But soon I will not be afraid to leave her sons with her long enough to learn their parents' ways. These are changing. Nobody who is comfortable and unafraid ever wants the risks and pains of war."

"Keep a man's belly full and you will have no trouble with him? Is that your thought, Bran—that a rich man can always buy peace?" An edge had come onto Matholuch's voice.

"Men whose bellies are full seldom leave their homes to fight," said Bran comfortably. "Only great fear or great wrath can make them do that, and such madness is usually the work of cunning liars. It is our business, my brothers Matholuch and Manawyddan, to see that no lies come between our two islands ever again. Let us drink to that."

The sons of Llyr drank, and Matholuch drank, shining-eyed; thinking how one day his son would be king of the Island of the Mighty. Heir to all the wealth of Bran.

Many days the men of the two islands feasted together in peace and gladness, but at last the time came when the Irish made ready to sail.

The day before that sailing, Manawyddan went to see Branwen his sister. She and her women were packing. He said, "Send these girls away, Branwen."

She did, then looked up at him wonderingly. "What is on you, Manawyddan?"

He put his hands on her shoulders. He held those two slim shoulders as if they were very precious things.

"Yourself, girl. This is your time to feel, and I am going to try to make you think."

She smiled up at him. "About what, brother? I am doing what Bran and the Council want, and I am happy."

"Happy? Branwen, girl, are you sure of that?"

She said simply, "Not altogether. You know that I could not be, brother. It is hard to leave my kin and my home and my friends, but who can have all she wants? I love my man, as our mother loved our father."

"You will be going far. Out of sight and reach of us all, with a man whom three moons ago you had never seen. Penardim did too much for Llyr, but never that."

She winced, but her eyes were steady. "I know what is in your mind, brother. Because he went away and had to be brought back, you do not trust him. You are hurt and angry, for me, as he was hurt and angry for the sake of his horses—those beautiful horses! But I trust him; I know he loves me."

"No doubt he does. You are the fairest of women. And you, because he is a fine figure of a man, you think his heart must be as fine. But such loving passes; like fire, it burns high, then burns out. Desire will come and go as long as your two bodies are healthy, but friendship and respect must be there always if a man and woman are to live happily together through the long years. Think, girl, before you go with this man! Do you respect him now as you did before Bran had to buy him back for you?"

She shrank, she stared past him. Trying to see, not that night of cold and loneliness and hurt, but Matholuch, only Matholuch, still warm, still magnificent, still hers.

"What kind of friend is he, girl? You have heard, from his own mouth. Once, I think, he hoped to gain power and glory through the Children of Llassar, but he forsook them at his people's bidding, as once already he has forsaken you. Will you give him another chance to do that?"

But now the picture he was drawing seemed too callous, too unlike the man she knew. She raised her head.

"He is my man," she said. "You forgive a child for forgetting love when it is hurt and angry, and I have forgiven him."

"Your man—yet a child? He can hardly be both."

She laughed softly, assured again. "What man is not, sometimes? There are times when every man needs the mother in his woman, maybe when every woman needs the father in her man. The Gods did not give us Their own strength, brother."

"True enough, but those times had better not come too often. You cannot be Matholuch's mother."

Branwen suddenly dimpled. "I do not want to be. Can one ever gain much without risking much? If the first woman who burned her fingers had put fire out of her house forever, what would we be doing now? Eating our meat raw, like beasts."

"You blind yourself, girl."

Again her smile flashed into dimpled wickedness. "Did she leave so sour a taste in your mouth, brother— that beautiful Queen in the south, of whom I have heard tell?"

Manawyddan said shortly, "He—or more likely she— lies who says that Rhiannon of the Birds ever loved any man but Pwyll, Prince of Dyved."

"Then how did she get her son—she who was childless so long that Pwyll's folk turned against her and told him that if she did not bear a child within twelve more moons they would not let him keep her? And that same year you visited Dyved, my brother, and somehow Rhiannon got her boy. Nor have you ever looked long upon any woman since, although you say that such fires always burn out."

Manawyddan laughed impatiently. "Every man in Dyved will tell you that young Pryderi is the image of his father Pwyll."

"Will they? Those who wish to can see great family likenesses between any two faces that each hold one nose and two eyes and one mouth."

"You tease me to keep away thought, girl."

"You too do not think of everything, Manawyddan." She was serious again, a grave-eyed queen. "It is too late now to speak against Matholuch. Our parting would be a fresh insult to him, one that might breed war."

"It would be no insult, girl. Bran would have to give him some more gifts; that is all. You are not property to be given away like the Cauldron; none can blame you if at the last you feel you cannot bear to go so far from home. Here the Old Tribes still rule, and we are the mightiest of the Islands of the Mighty; no smaller isle will send an invading host against us."

Branwen said, "I cannot be happy without Matholuch."

Manawyddan's hands dropped. "Then may you be happy with him, little sister! None wishes that more than I."

With her Irishman Branwen sailed from Aber Menai. From the shore the sons of Llyr watched her go. The day was gray; the heavens brooded low, like vast, sad-colored wings, upon the earth. As long as she could see them Branwen looked back at her brothers; they looked at her until she shrank to the size of a child, dwindled to the size of a doll. At last only the ships were left, toy-sized, passing down into the gray maw of the mists. Distance, the witch that has power to make the greatest small, had swallowed them up.

The sons of Llyr went back to Harlech, and most of the way they were silent. Once Bran said heavily, "What will the girl look like, suckling her own baby? It seems only the day before yesterday that she herself was nursing at our mother's breast. I wish Ireland were nearer, or that we were not such busy men, and could go there oftener. Say what you are thinking, Manawyddan, I know well that you are thinking it: that I never should have let her go."

Manawyddan said, "I will not say it. She is gone now. But I too wish that Ireland were nearer. She said that the man was like a child. Well, every woman must keep in practice for motherhood, and she is wise as well as foolish. But it is a man's business to be a man."

5

The Blow

Matholuch brought Branwen to Tara, and they were welcomed there with joy that blazed like fire, and was louder than song. The New Tribes were glad to see their King back in triumph, and the Old Tribes were glad because the new Queen was of their blood, and might make their lot easier. Branwen's beauty and treasures dazzled all; Bran had given her great wealth with which to win friends. The *Mabinogi* says that for a whole year not one chief or lady that visited her came away without a jewel of great price.

Then her son was born, Gwern the son of Matholuch. The King swelled with pride. His dreams were becoming flesh and blood. What an unheard of great kingdom might be built were both islands to become the boy's heritage!

Subtly and cautiously he began to work toward that end. He spoke to Amergin the High Druid, the oldest and wisest man in Ireland. But Amergin said, "No son has ever followed his father in Tara. Men of your tribe

took it from the Priest-Kings of old, those God-chosen
ones who were named when we druids sang a Spell
of Truth over a sleeping man, and he in his dream
beheld the King that was to be. But you New Tribes
made Tara the prize of the strongest; he became king
who killed the king. Until your uncle died in his bed,
and you said that the Gods had taken him because it
was time for you, his sister's son, to wear his crown.
A good change, and one that fitted our ancient laws.
It is soon to make another."

Matholuch smiled; he gave Amergin and all the
druids great gifts. "Times change rapidly nowadays.
Go read your stars; I think they will tell you that
Gwern my son will be the best High King the Irish have
ever had."

They went, but they came back grave-faced. Amergin
said, "Evil will it be for Ireland, Lord, if your son is
ever king. Evil that will be remembered to the end of
life and time."

Matholuch paled. "Why? What will happen?"

For a breath's space Amergin hesitated, then he said,
"Lord, why vex your heart with woes that need never
come? No man is the better for black visions. Let your
boy be reared here, learning to love Ireland and the
Irish, then go home to be king in his uncle's land.
So, and so only, will your marriage bear good fruit."

Wrath flamed in Matholuch's face. "Do the stars
say that? Or is that your own word, old man?"

But the steady eyes of Amergin met his, and the
King's eyes fell. Later he said to Branwen, "We must
go slowly. In time these old men without vision will die
off, and with them the grudges they nurse. Meantime I
will be winning over the younger druids. You too must
keep on giving gifts, Branwen."

"I will. But," her face was troubled, "what did the
Lord Amergin read in the stars? He is old and wise."

He laughed shortly. "Druids' wisdom and your Ancient Harmonies! Both are old wives' tales, woman."

She winced and thought, *His rearing speaks. The ways of the New Tribes. Not his own nature.*

He went on. "In the end I will get my way. I have before. Unless," and he frowned "the people should get to know of the insult your brother Evnissyen put on me. That my war chiefs would never brook."

She winced again. "But they must know of that already. All your men knew, that sailed with you."

"The druids I had with me laid it upon them as *gessa* not to speak of it. Or of the Cauldron. Your brother made me a two-edged gift there, woman. What use is victory if one must be torn limb from limb by one's own victorious warriors when they can find no more foes to kill?"

"My brother paid you the best face-price he could, Lord. Not many kings would have given up that Cauldron."

"I know that, woman. I have never denied it."

But he did not laugh and kiss her as once he would have. He was used to her now, and no longer a great lover by day. But Gwern crowed and held up chubby hands to her, and Branwen cuddled him and was content. She knew that when night came his father would need and love her again.

He did. That night, and for many nights. She was watching herself for signs of another conception when Amergin died. Many wept, for Amergin had guided Erin long and well; he had been the last pillar of a golden age that was gone, the last shield of the Old Tribes. Mighty were his funeral games; mightier than would have been held for any other man save the King. And the night those games ended, one of the men who had sailed with Matholuch got drunk and talked. Maybe with the High Druid dead the ancient terrible bonds of *gessa* seemed less frightening, maybe too some of the lesser druids worked on him, fearing the King who had new ideas and wanted to open up new roads. Anyhow he did talk, and though the Gods may have attended to him thereafter, the men of Ireland attended to Matholuch.

All over the land a cry of rage went up. From every chief who had the blood of the New Tribes in his veins.

"Lord, you have reddened the face of all Ireland!"

"That outland King was spitting on you! You have let him send you home like a beaten pup, with a few pitiful bones in your mouth—you, the High King of Ireland! We are ashamed to hold our heads up."

"You should have got that Evnissyen's head, and you have not got even one ear off it!"

When the King went out in his chariot, refined people looked the other way, and the vulgar jeered and spat at him. The harassed man no longer had friends or kinsmen or subjects; he had only a swarm of maddened hornets. Or rather, they had him. They buzzed in his ears, and at last they buzzed inside his head. And always, underneath all, were the words that were never spoken, yet rang loudest in his ears: *Lord, you had not the courage to try to take the head of him that shamed you. Lord, you are a coward.*

Branwen was his only comfort. Her tender arms and white breast, her clear shining eyes and soft voice that still admired and praised him, a great man whose clear-headedness and farsightedness his people could not understand. When he came to her sore and humiliated he went away feeling noble; well puffed up again. He even tried using some of her arguments in the council chamber, but his councilors sneered at him.

"Lord, you have been lessoned by a woman. The

Queen is bound to defend her own people, but honor leaves the man who is a woman's tool."

Matholuch began to wonder, *Is she speaking from her heart when she praises me? Which does she love more—me or the princes of the greater Island of the Mighty?*

After that he sometimes spoke harshly to her, and seemed to blame her for his troubles. But at others his need made him cling to her. Branwen bore his tempers as she would have borne her child's had he been sick. She hoped that the storm would pass.

But it did not. It grew. In every breeze the people seemed to hear the laughter of the men of the greater island, mocking them whose King they had belittled. Any people can be worked up, or down, into a mob; and a mob must have something to tear. In the end they had an idea. It may have been hatched in the brain of some unworthy druid, cunning replacing the wisdom that had died with Amergin.

A deputation came to Matholuch; too many great men for the King's comfort. Some of them seemed to want to look the other way, but their spokesman faced him squarely.

"Lord, these are our terms. Take them or leave them."

Matholuch looked at them, and his face was stony and calm, as became a king. But his eyes were green and shifty, like the eyes of a cornered fox.

"What is it you ask?" he said.

"This, Lord. That you put away the woman you have with you, Branwen the daughter of Llyr, the sister of the King of the other Island of the Mighty."

There was a brief pause; the King moistened his lips. He said, "Very well. The woman is a good woman, yet her going is not too great a thing to grant to make my people happy. I love them more." He thought,

Branwen loves me. She will make a fuss about this, but what is one more fuss among so many? She will not make it to her brother; she will not want him coming after my head.

Easy for her to say that she went home of her own accord, because she was homesick; to the Old Tribes that would seem natural enough.

The man answered, "Lord, we will not let her go. We have not got her brother, who reddened your face for you, and all Ireland's through you, but we have got her. This is what we will do." And they told him.

In her Sunny Chamber Branwen heard those terms before the King himself heard them. Her women watched her face hungrily while they told her, as a hawk watches chickens. With a consuming eagerness to pounce and pierce, and miss nothing that they could tell other people about afterward.

She laughed a little. She said, "You are dreaming."

They shook their heads, their eyes shining. "No. It is true. Lady, we grieve for you."

She knew that they did not. She knew well, now, how much friendship her gifts had bought her. For many long days these talebearers had been besieging her, telling her everything they heard and a good deal more, and trying to make her talk about it. That they had to make up nearly all the answers that they repeated to others as hers was perhaps a slight nuisance to them, and her one comfort. She was a queen bred in queenliness; she never had shown temper or fear.

But she was also young, and alone under many hostile eyes, and now at last she had to admit to herself that she was afraid. Not of these foolish threats, of course; Matholuch never would let anyone touch her. But what humiliation it must be for him to have to listen to such shameful proposals. That his men should dare! Never could such a thing have happened in her own Island of the Mighty.

This was her fear, one that made her heart beat so hard that she was afraid all these greedily watching women might hear it—what if Matholuch lost his temper with these traitors? What if they should hurt him?

She wondered; she became a flame and an intensity of wonder: how was he facing them? Easy, so easy, to picture how her brothers would have faced them: Bran with a great bellow that would have blown them all out of his presence, their hair standing on end; Manawyddan with a few cold words as quiet as steady, even rainfall, as crushing as hail. His voice would have been the coldest thing in the world, and it would have chilled them to the bone.

But how would Matholuch, her own man, face them? Carefully she locked and bolted the doors of her mind against any notion that he was less of a man than her brothers, but she was afraid. What if he should go mad and splutter? Then they would mock at him and humiliate him, and he had already been so much humiliated . . .

She rose. She could not keep still any longer. She said, "If the men have gone I will go to the King and ask him what they really did say. You have made me curious."

They smiled; they thought that she was afraid for herself. And so she left them, never dreaming that it was for the last time.

Silence greeted her in the corridors. As many silences as there were people, and as many qualities of silence, all weaving themselves together into one great silence. Once someone tittered, but she turned and stared that mocker back into silence, her eyes the eyes of Llyr as long ago he had faced Eurosswydd in the Red Man's hall.

She came to the council chamber, she knocked on the door and waited for an answer. None came, and she opened it. Matholuch sat inside, very still. He did not move or look at her.

She stared at him and could not find him. His face was once again an obstacle, a painted, carved mask hung between him and her. So much familiar jut of nose, so much brightish beard below eyes that now were gray as faded, sunless water. Eyes that avoided hers, nose that jutted purposefully into nothingness, beard behind which his jaw had always lain hid.

She stared at him as though she would throw out all her soul through her eyes, to pierce the shield of that face and find the man hiding beneath it. And in that very hiding—not in any reaching of him that hid there—found at last her answer.

An answer that seemed to open the earth beneath her, to send her sliding down into a limitless gray abyss. So far down that her outreaching hands never again could come at anything warm and human forever. And as she sank into that awful solitude memories mocked her, whirling shapes of what had been, voices crying for the last time as they vanished into nothingness, *"Branwen! Branwen, daughter of Llyr!"* Her girlhood in the Island of the Mighty, and all the tenderness and joy. All the pride in her, and all the hope that she, the strong and beautiful, might lie with heroes and bear the mighty ones of the earth.

This was the man she had loved, and allowed to father her child! This was her shame, and the shame of the Island of the Mighty! *But most of all your shame, your sorrow, Branwen, you who are alone.*

Matholuch stirred, and he looked uneasily at his feet and said, "Go away, Branwen. I will talk to you later."

He never meant to see her again. He did not want to face her. Clearly, in that last hour of their life together, she saw him and understood. It was not that he wished her ill. For a little while he would miss her—it would be hard to find as fair a woman for his bed. So little she mattered to him, or any other woman, save as they touched his comfort.

Her face turned red and then white again. She laughed, an awful laugh, like the sound of a heart breaking, and cried out at him.

"Oh, Matholuch of the Mouse's Heart, it is more shame to me to lie in a coward's bed than in his kitchen. That is my disgrace and my sorrow that there is no amending—that ever I should have lain with you!"

Matholuch sprang up and struck her in the face. Red came out on her cheek and delicate ear, but still she laughed.

That was the first blow that ever was struck Branwen, but it was very far from being the last.

They set her in the big, waist-high pit where the cooking was done. They set the huge cooking spit itself upon her shoulders, so that she had to bow beneath it, sweating in the heat of the flames. Every day for three years she, who had been Queen in Tara, toiled there in its kitchen, a drudge. And every day the butcher came and gave her a box on the ear; people came from far to see that, and to laugh.

"As her people have reddened the Goddess Ireland's face, so let her face be reddened!"

Quiet years those were outside the kitchen, quiet in both islands. The *Mabinogi* says that his men said to Matholuch, "Lord, forbid all ships to sail to the Island of the Mighty, and all folk that come from there, let them not go back again to make this thing known," and that the King obeyed them; once again the head of the dog had become its well-wagged tail. But it seems more likely that he sent false messages to her brothers in Branwen's name. So long a silence surely would have waked suspicion in the sons of Llyr.

6

Branwen and the Starling

If Branwen had any consolations during those years we are not told of them. She had hard work to do, and that must have been the least of her torments, and her only salvation.

Eyes and hands and tongues jabbing at her like wasps; curiously, ceaselessly, greedily, with a vicious playfulness. There is always a bit of Evnissyen in every mob.

An outland woman alone among enraged and outraged this-landers; a Queen handed over to scullions crazed with excitement by the very height and depth of her fall, so that class took revenge upon class. The doom of the daughter of Llyr.

The women must have harassed her in many little ways. The men may have pawed and leered. She may have learned to sleep with the kitchen spit in her hand, perhaps with water boiling on the kitchen fire beside her; water that the women would spill on her if they could . . . Not good to look too long into abysses or to try to plumb their fetid depths.

Branwen set her teeth and bore all. Never should these outlanders see her weep. All that they could do she could endure and live through; never would she ask mercy. *They* would ask it—easy enough, when the time came, to shame them as they never had been able to shame her.

In all save one thing. One red scar, one fouling shame, of which she never could be free until she was rid of the soiled body that had betrayed her.

She had loved Matholuch; her flesh had responded to his flesh . . .

That was what sometimes, when her aching head rang with all the whirling, maddening noise of the great kitchen, almost broke her—hours once sweet that burned her memory now more than the butcher's hard palm could burn her skin. Times that made it seem not worthwhile to fight, to try to save anything so cheapened, so degraded as herself.

Do you want your kin and your friends and the whole Isle of the Mighty to know what you loved—how he loved you, the beautiful, the proud? It is not pleasant to be pitied when you have been proud. Here at least you are not pitied.

And she was not; that was very true.

Die and let the earth hide your shame. Help could not bring back happiness to you, only expose that shame.

She gritted her teeth and said to herself, I will not break. I am a princess of the Isle of the Mighty, and before I am that I am a person, and I will do the duty of both. There is my baby. I gave him the Mouse-heart for a father; I must not wrong him more. I must see to it that my blood rules in him, not theirs.

Time must have eased her lot a little. One grows

used to anything, also her humiliation had gone on so long that it was no longer a show. People no longer came to the kitchen to watch and jeer, people who once would have been glad to boast of a word or a glance from her; and her fellow servants grew used to her being there. Since she did no spiteful acts herself, some even began to feel a secret, sneaking pity for her.

Once, as they worked together, a woman whispered, "Your boy is in fosterage among the best men of Ireland." She named the place. "They make much of him there. The King and his Council still hope to get good from your people through him."

That was the one bright day in all those long dark years. But Branwen could not even whisper back her thanks. She saw the head steward watching them, her implacable foe, and had to stare coldly and turn her back. The woman either did not understand or understood too well and was afraid; she offered no more kindnesses. She finally rejoined the ranks of Branwen's tormentors.

Days and weeks, and moons and years. Lying down each night exhausted and waking each morning to know that the butcher would come, and that somebody would laugh.

Once when all were sleeping she rose and went out into the night. The wind was cool on her bruised face. The moon was full, and she looked at it, wondering at the vast peace of the cloudy sky. She bathed her soul in the stillness, that after the daylong torture in the hot, noisy kitchen was sweeter to her than music.

In the eaves of the palace there was a starlings' nest; now a faint cry came from below it. A small cry, a bird's cry, but it shattered the stillness. Pain was back in the world again. Branwen moved toward it. She thought, *Maybe this once I can turn aside the whip.*

She found a fledgling fluttering and crying, and the

cat watching it, green-eyed. Blood showed, where already the cat had pounced once.

Ordinarily the cat and Branwen were good friends; it was the one inmate of the kitchen that never had mocked or hurt her. Often she had fed and stroked it on the sly, afraid that if she were seen to fondle the beast it would be made to suffer. But she had no mind to let her friend have this living meal. She snatched up the fledgling and carried it back to the kitchen, where she got water to bathe the wound, that was not deep. The cat came after her and mewed plaintively, rubbing against her legs, unable to understand her unkindness, but she paid no heed. She put the bird in the hollow of her kneading trough, and tended it there, a dark little puff of down with red blood running down one half-feathered wing.

She said, when the wound was staunched, "I have done all I can. You must live or die now, as the Mothers will." And she carried it back, but the nest was too high for her to reach. Then, harder than the butcher's palm, a thought smote her, sharp and dazzling as lightning in the black night.

Lightning indeed, cleaving long night . . .

The starlings that Penardim our mother used to keep! How we used to love to teach them to talk, and we little! It is a sign. It is the road—my road! My chance, at last.

She carried the small starling back to the kneading trough, and she gave the cat cream, reckless for once as to whether it would be missed or not. "You have served me," she whispered into those furry ears, "served me well, whether you meant to or not, and it has been long since anyone did that."

In the morning the butcher was there to strike her again before the grinning servants, though fewer may have sniggered than at first. The sight was an old story now.

But now she had a refuge—something to do besides bracing herself against the trough and making a blank of her face.

She had hope. There in the trough she had wings, and they would grow and strengthen until they grew great enough to fly across the sea to the Island of the Mighty.

She had a tongue beside her tongue, and in the end it would pierce her enemies like a spear.

She was a smith, and that tongue was the sword she was forging. She was a poet, and it was her pupil.

She became as wily as a serpent, as persistent as death. She worked slowly, for sureness, for safety. They must never suspect, never guess what she was about, there in the kitchen of Matholuch.

At night she trained the bird, whispering softly into its feathers while others slept. Sometimes she took it out into the darkness, where she could speak louder and it, too, could learn how to pitch its voice and articulate clearly in the alien tongue of men.

She packed it with words, and she packed it with food, that turned into strength and size and muscle, into the strength for rising immense distances, for flight . . .

It thrived, there in the kneading trough. It forgot the nest and knew only her. Sometimes it would reach up and peck her fingers caressingly, then take a bite or two of dough before settling back again into the hollow.

We do not know how she kept it from speaking in the daytime, or how she taught it where it must go. In those days when the subtle senses were not yet lost, when the walls between the worlds were not yet so firm but that outlaws like Llassar and his wife could flee from one to the other, and thicken and harden into earth's denser mold, understanding may have been easier between men and birds.

Nor do we know the full powers of her royal druid line . . .

The *Mabinogi* says she taught it what kind of man Bran her brother was, so she must have been able to make pictures pass from her mind to that small mind.

Summer came; sap flowed like holy blood, quickening the veins of earth. The trees were full of life, green life and singing life, the sky smiled, and the starling grew restless. Branwen saw that she was old enough to fly.

The discovery was delight, and it was terror. It was an end . . .

She had had hope, she had had suspense, she had had an end to work toward. Now she would still have hope and a far greater suspense, but again she would wait helpless, with bound hands.

How long—how long, O Mothers—before she can reach Bran? And then how long—how long—before Bran can come? Wait—and wait—and wait—and then perhaps he will never come. A hawk may take the starling, or storms drown her in the sea, or she may forget all and follow a lover, as once you followed one, Branwen, daughter of Llyr!

All one night she crouched under the stars, the starling against her breast. She talked to it, she muttered charms that later men would call mesmeric. She poured power out of herself, she could feel mind and will flowing out of her like blood, into that little feathered shape.

Dawn came. Age seized upon the night, all her years came at once upon that proud sweet darkness, and upon the world. Her black hair turned gray, trailed its dead wan ghastliness upon the earth. The east whitened, then began to bleed, like a woman's smitten face.

Branwen rose. One last time she repeated her speech to the bird. One last time it repeated her words to her.

She held up her hands to the east, the bird in them, she kissed its head, and threw it into the air. It sped away like an arrow, straight toward the Island of the Mighty.

Branwen looked after it, then suddenly burst into tears. "O my bird, it is long and hard, the journey that is before you! I never should have let you go!"

She had sent away the one friend of her loneliness; she had won its love, then used it as a tool.

And that was the first time in more than three years that Branwen, daughter of Llyr, had wept.

Long and lonely was the bird's flight. She was young, and she never had flown far before. She saw strange fields green beneath her, and she saw the different, grayer green of the Irish Sea, stirring constantly and softly, like a great snake. She feared that bleak vastness, she who never had seen more water than that in the horse trough, or in a puddle at the kitchen door.

She flew on.

She flew until she was so tired that it seemed she must drop into the sea, until her wings were heavy as stones and her eyes began to make their own night.

Then a wind blew in her face, a warm wind, sweet with the scent of green, succulent growing things. The good smell of earth again, and trees, trees on which a tired bird could perch. She was hungry and worn out, and she smelled food and rest.

But the wind beat her back, it blew her this way and that. She had to fight against it, beating her tired wings against the shining air.

Cliffs rose out of the sea, gray and stark, and again

her heart rose. Solidness to perch on. Blessed rest, blessed freedom from upholding the weary weight of oneself . . .

Then she saw great birds, far bigger than herself, wheeling and circling round those cliffs. Their screams smote her ears like the very voice of death.

One had seen her and was speeding toward her, his long neck outstretched, his black eyes glinting, his beak shining, greedy, cruel as death.

With a scream of her own she turned and fled seaward again, back toward the death of weariness, the drop into the cold gaping waters that at least would have no beak to tear one with, no fierce greedy eyes to gloat while that beak tore one's flesh.

But she was tired, too tired. And the gull was swift. It headed her off; she saw another coming, hovering there above the sea.

She turned back and dived lower, in one last frantic burst of speed, looking madly for some crevice in the cliffs to hide in, some little place where no bird of prey might follow.

She found none.

But she saw something else—a boat below her, piled with fish, such as sometimes they brought into the kitchen at home for Branwen to cook. Two men were on it. She dropped, plummet-like, on the far side of that pile of fish, away from the men.

The gull swooped after her. But the men thought it was after the fish and shouted, and one waved a coat at it while the other snatched up a piece of wood to throw.

The gull rose and flew away.

They did not see her, hiding among the fish. She crouched there and shivered, exhausted; her heart beat like a hammer, as if it were trying to smash through her breast.

The boat came to shore. In a quiet, green place in the cliff walls, where there were no gulls. Her heart had steadied somewhat; she set herself, rose and was off through the air in a magnificent, painful burst of speed. She heard a voice call out behind her, but no stone whizzed through the air.

She reached the shore. She flew on, straight as a cast spear, a miserable and frightened and gallant little spear, looking for trees. She found them finally; what bliss it was to feel their green, blessed shade close her! Her feet closed upon a branch, and so upon heaven; her tired wings rested, furled at last . . .

She woke; she ate and attended to her feathers. Sleep came once more, like a great, dark, soft wing . . .

She woke again, and remembered Branwen.

She flew on, over this strange island in which she had not been hatched, looking for the man who was not to be feared because he was kind to all things, the man whose image Branwen had made her see.

The *Mabinogi* says that Bran was at Caer Seiont, in Arvon, and by that it probably means Caer Seon, later to be the lordship of Gwydion the Golden-Tongued, Gwydion the son of Don. Then it must have belonged to Math the Ancient, that great king who was so mighty a man of illusion and fantasy that only two men born ever can have equalled him: Gwydion, his own nephew and pupil, and that far-famed Merlin who in a later age was to make Arthur king of Britain. Most likely it was in counsel, not in goods, that Math paid tribute to Bran the High King.

Bran must have been sitting in front of Caer Seon, for he could not have got inside it, and there must have been other men with him.

The starling saw him, and she saw them.

She wanted to go to him at once, but she was afraid; one of those other men might be a stone-thrower. She had learned fear too well, in this vast, windy world outside the kitchen, to take many chances.

She perched upon the nearest tree: she found a bug and ate it. She waited, brown eyes fixed on Bran.

If only those other men would go away . . . !

They did not, and the day wore. The blue faded from the sky; the sun slanted downward, fire-red, in the bloody west.

Night is coming, and I will get sleepy. I must get to him, and make the noises she taught me. Before I am too sleepy to remember.

With a wild cry of fear at her own daring, she sailed through the air; made her landing in the only place where it seemed likely that she could keep her footing if he tried to shake her off. Among the stuff that was like thick, queer-colored grass on top of his great head.

A man or two cried out, but Math the Ancient lifted his hand; the hand that had such mysterious might.

"There is meaning in this," he said.

"There is something in it," said Bran. "I am taller than other men, but it is not usual for birds to come and sit on me."

He reached up gently, and the bird recognized that gentleness. She let his great hand close upon her and lift her down. He held her so that their eyes met.

"Little one," he said, "I am not a tree. It may be that you thought so and have made a mistake. Or again it may be that you have a good reason for coming to perch on me?"

He may have thought her no true bird, but a man or woman bewitched.

What Math the Ancient thought no man knew. He stared into the bloodstained golden west, and in his face was the sadness of a god; of one who beholds an oncoming darkness vaster than night, far more terrible than night . . .

Bran looked at the bird, and the bird looked at Bran. Her beak opened; from it came a squeaky echo of Branwen's voice of beauty. "Bran—Bran son of Llyr—greetings from Branwen, daughter of Llyr . . ."

That night found Bran already on his way back to Harlech, and signal fires blazing from the hills, like fallen stars.

7

The Hosting of the Island of the Mighty

Before the folk of fourscore and seven counties Bran told what Branwen suffered; and from side to side of the great rock his voice rolled as though the thunder had forsaken the clouds of heaven to find an earthly home and issuing place in his breast.

The people heard; their whole beings quivered like the strings of smitten harps. A red cloud, too fine for any but druid sight, covered Harlech; the airy beings, the Elementals that feed on blood, hovered in it, sniffing hopefully at those fumes of dark promise.

Ireland! Ireland! That was the name gabbled on all tongues, cried in all hearts. As a pack of starving dogs hungers for meat, they hungered to get there. *Ireland! . . . Ireland . . . Branwen! Branwen, daughter of Llyr!*

As wind fans flames, so Bran and Manawyddan fanned that blaze. They themselves were burning; for them there could be no rest until their bodies should be in Ireland with Branwen, where their minds already hovered, impotent, fleshless shades.

So ended the Golden Age of the Island of the Mighty, the peace of Bran the Blessed.

That night in council it was decided how many men should go with the High-King into Ireland, and how many should stay at home. No doubt the strongest and bravest went with Bran, those with the finest bodies and often the finest minds. In war the first-goers are always the fittest fathers of the future, perhaps not only of men, but also of poetry and thought. Our world might have been darker had Homer not been blind.

Another decision was made in that council, and in the morning it was proclaimed before the people.

Seven chiefs were named to hold the Island of the Mighty in the absence of her King. And the seventh and chief over the other six, for all his youth, was Caradoc, son of Bran.

The naming of that name made silence; silence deep as that at the bottom of a well.

A light kindled on many faces among the New Tribes. *Bran never would do this if he did not want Caradoc to be King after him. The Isle is turning from its old ways. To ours!*

The Old Tribes stood mute, dazed as men might be who, while sitting quietly at home, suddenly see and hear a great wind wrench away a wall or a ceiling.

Eyes moved with an incredible, covert activity. Eyes that were questions, eyes that were hopes and fears and suspicions. Eyes that held merely blank bewilderment.

A man with a rich uncle thought, *If Caradoc can be King after Bran, will I get my uncle's fields when he dies? Or will Kilydd and Kai get them, Kilydd and Kai that are probably his sons?*

A man with a rich father thought, *Will I be able to get Glelwyd's lands after him—and laugh at those sniggering sons of his sister, that think they will be so much richer than I?*

Doors opening everywhere, upon unheard of vistas, doors slamming shut upon the old and the safe and the known . . .

Many tried to think that surely Bran did not mean to make so great a change, that things would settle back into their old shape and be the same when he came home from Ireland. But the heart of every man who wished to inherit from his uncle grew cold within him, and the blood of every son who would have liked to inherit from his father quickened and grew hot in his veins.

But the sons of Beli stood like an island within an island, no light on their faces, their eyes dull as storm clouds. Only the eyes of Caswallon, eldest and ablest of them, began to smolder . . .

Young Pryderi of Dyved laughed and clapped Caradoc on the shoulder. "A good choice, son of Bran the Blessed, and may his blessedness be with you!"

He was the first to break that silence, and his word was the word of a chief.

All applauded then; Bran the King had spoken, and his will would be done. The Old Tribes, who alone might have wished to oppose him, had no other leader. Besides, they were divided against themselves, nephews and sons.

Only Manawyddan, son of Llyr, kept silence, and Math the Much-Born, the son of Mathonwy.

That decision truly had been reached earlier, while the King was waiting for his people to come in. Only the four sons of dark Penardim had been there, and Math the Ancient.

Bran had unfolded his plan, and Evnissyen had leaned forward, his face twisted with savage glee.

"That is good to hear. Never then will the Island of the Mighty come under the foul spawn of that outland dog!"

"Be still," said Manawyddan, "you who dug the pit they have put our sister into. And do not misname her son."

"He is the seed of Matholuch. A shame to her, and a danger to us! And did I make Matholuch a coward and a traitor? Is his baseness my doing?"

"We have no right to speak before our elders, brother," said Nissyen. "We who are the youngest here."

Manawyddan looked at him. "And what would you say, brother Nissyen?"

Nissyen said softly, "Sorrow and sorrow and sorrow. For Evnissyen's insult that brought her to this, and for hers that takes us to her in Ireland."

"You mean that now we are insulted as the men of Ireland were insulted, so that to go in wrath is only to keep the Wheel turning? I know that. I know that soon even our own men will be thinking less of her than of Irish heads on a pole. But Branwen is there: what else can we do?"

"Nothing," said Nissyen. "Nothing now."

Evnissyen showed his teeth at him in an evil snarling smile. "This is once when you will not be able to make peace—milk-drinker! And do not tell me again to be silent! Your time for speech is past, and you never did deeds. You are only a cloak over nothing. A wind would blow you away."

"It is I who bade you be silent," said Manawyddan, and though his voice was not loud, Evnissyen suddenly became still. Manawyddan looked at Bran. "I will not say again what I have said before, brother. How will Beli's sons take this? And Branwen herself, when we set her free? She has borne enough sorrow without your disinheriting her son. She bears it still."

He ceased, and in the silence all her brothers could hear the slap of the butcher's hand against Branwen's cheek. Remembered that it was not long until morning . . .

Bran said heavily, "You are always telling me to remember the good of the people, Manawyddan. And I have remembered. Branwen's son is the son of Matholuch, and can I trust the Island of the Mighty to the seed of a traitor? Of the man who has dealt with her as he has dealt with her?" His great hands clenched on the rock beneath him, so that a little of it crumbled in his fingers.

"The Mothers bear me witness, brother, that I wish the little boy all good—he is her son, and I am ready to love him for her sake—but to give him the Island of the Mighty is daring much. You may say, 'Wait and try him,' but how can we ever be sure? His father is fair and false. And I shall have Ireland to leave him— the land he was born in."

For what seemed a long time Manawyddan sat silent. Far below the gulls cried, and somewhere among the tents a sleeping man cried out, in the grip of evil dreams.

"There is some right with you, my brother," he said at last, "and that makes you more wrong. Your wrath against Matholuch is strong, and weds a new excuse to your old desire. Would that the veil of the Mothers still held, and that we men had never learned that we could father sons! I see that Math here is right in trying to keep that knowledge out of Gwynedd as long as he can. Without it you would see only Branwen in her baby, and we should still have peace to come home to."

"Matholuch would still be in him," said Bran.

"That is true, too," said Manawyddan, and sighed. "But there is good and evil in every man. All men must clean the evil out of themselves, no matter how many lives it takes. So the druids teach, and so we believe. And I think, brother, that we could teach any son of Branwen's, conceived while she loved the father, to manifest the good in himself oftener than the bad."

"The Island of the Mighty is a great trust," said Bran.

"Is that why you will bring a new kind of war upon it? One that will only be beginning when we come home? Those of us who do come home . . ."

Bran looked toward Math. "What is your word, son of great Mathonwy? Are you with my brother, Manawyddan, son of Llyr, or with me? You have lived longer than either of us; long before we were born men called you wise."

Math raised his eyes then, those gray eyes that seemed infinite as the stream of time itself, upon which floats all that has been and all that is. So vast his vision seemed, and so different were his eyes from the eyes of common men. Their greatness was equalled only by their sadness, the sadness of the farseeing.

"Does it matter," he said at last, "what my counsel is? For the old calm world of which we are the pillars is breaking, and a new world shaping. Old days and old ways are passing. Here is an end. For awhile longer I shall keep the peace in Gwynedd, but he that comes after me shall break it. For even Gwynedd that I have tried to keep remote from the turmoil of men is bread baking in the oven of the fates—already the stuff strains against me and tries to rise and escape from the shape into which I would knead it.

"And that is part of the Great Going-Forward. There can be no stopping; the world grows as a child grows, and no man is ever full-grown. He dies when the time comes for him to grow somewhere else.

"We have been guardians of earth's babyhood, kings who were fathers of the people, and the world would be happier if we could remain the only fathers. But now mankind must grow up, and each man find and train the King within himself. That is as it should be. To depend upon a leader is to fail to develop one's own strength or to strive for clear vision. He that fights must lead or obey a leader; only he that is strong enough to stand alone can stay at peace."

Bran leaned forward eagerly. "Then change is good in the end? If it brings evil for a time, that is only like a woman's birth pangs?"

"If it comes too fast it can bring long evil," said Math, "evil that will outlast all the birth pangs ever borne."

"You think that I bring it too fast?"

"If I said so, would you turn from the path on which your heart drives you? The path that maybe is destiny? Already, too, it may be too late to turn back. You have sent your sister away, you have lit the signal fires upon the hills."

Bran's great hands clenched again. "The Mothers know that if I could undo what I have done I never would let Branwen go from us! But the signal fires upon the hills," and his voice was as the deep growl of a lion sunk in this throat, "them I would light again! Men, they hold her there, bearing such shame and misery as among the Old Tribes never was inflicted upon any woman, queen or serf . . . Branwen! Our Branwen!" And he turned away his face.

Maybe Math thought of dark-eyed Don, his own sister, back at Caer Seon. He said gently, "True. The evil stinks to heaven. Yet Manawyddan and Nissyen and I could have gone into Ireland secretly and freed her.

Against my Illusion no Irishman but Amergin could have fought, and had he lived this black folly never would have been. Your sister would still lie in Matholuch's bed."

Evnissyen gasped with fury that broke all bonds. "You would take no revenge? *Bear* the insult?"

Manawyddan and Bran stared at him in wonder. Only in Nissyen's eyes was there understanding; he smiled faintly, with quiet sadness.

"Many women of the Island of the Mighty must weep now, for sons and brothers and lovers. Is Branwen's reddened face worth that?" Math's voice was as calm as ever.

"All the peoples of the mainland would laugh at us, hearing that I let my sister be used like a dog."

"Can strength never afford to be laughed at? You fight the New Tribes with their own weapons. Already you have forgotten ours."

"War is evil," said Manawyddan, "but this one has been forced upon us. You yourself have fought, Math, when Gwynedd was invaded."

"And will again. Yet war itself, not any race or tribe, is the enemy that shall pull down all that we of the Old Tribes have built. Among us neither man nor woman was ever master; all walked free. Women created property; they brought houses and tilled fields into being, because they needed shelter in which to rear their children, and food that would not fail when the day's hunting or fishing failed. They could leave little to chance, unlike man the free, the roaming hunter. So ownership, one of her children, has always descended through the line of the woman. And for long she ruled the folk she gathered together."

Bran and Manawyddan looked at each other, and nodded. In Ireland itself, the triumphant New Tribes never had been able to blot out the memory that Tara and all the other great Irish strongholds had been founded by women.

Math went on. "But war came—for new peoples came, and it will always be the instinct of the hungry to take from those who have food. And men made better war chiefs, better defenders. A war leader with a heavy child in her belly is not much good.

"Yet woman, though she ceased to be a king* and man protected her, was still reverenced as the source of life. Only now when man is learning that she cannot give life without him does he begin to scorn her whom he protects. So she that created property will become property.

"So it is already in the Eastern World, so it will be here. And out of that constant injustice will rise continually more evils to breed wars and fresh injustice until men forget that there was ever a world at peace. When humankind lets one half of humankind be enslaved it will be long and long, even when that slavery wanes, before freedom is respected and nation ceases to tear nation; before the world unlearns the habit of force."

He ceased, and great Bran drew a deep breath.

"If I can prevent that, nothing else matters. Tell me what to do, wise son of Mathonwy, and I will do it."

"I can make no promises," said Math. "Already the evil is conceived, and the world labors toward the misbegotten birth."

Bran looked at him and past him, and into the gray mists that overhung the sea. Dawn was coming, the pale sickly dawn of a day that would bring no happiness. In that paling darkness that was not light they all

---

*See Rhys, *Celtic Folklore*, p. 661, for probability that the Celtic title generally rendered "king" was once applicable to either sex. Also Macalister's *Tara* for Irish foundation legends.

looked into each other's faces and found no help; only wan, featureless masks.

Bran sighed. "It is not good that you see before the world, son of Mathonwy. It is a bitter thing to know that all this will come upon the folk, and that they must go backward instead of forward. Or at least go forward by a very roundabout way.

"Yet you that see so much—dare I ask you what you see for Branwen my sister? And for Caradoc my son?"

Again Math looked at him with those gray eyes that now seemed to unite in one the whole trinity of time—past, present and to be.

"I cannot see so clearly as that, son of Llyr. I can hear the cries of many that will be slain, and smell the blood that is not yet shed, but that is the fate of the many. For the few, those that I myself know, my heart blinds my druid sight."

Evnissyen laughed. "Well, that is one thing to be thankful for, Lord of Gwynedd. It is the first cheerful thing you have said."

Math turned his eyes upon him. "Even energy that has been turned to pure evil has its part in the pattern," he said. "But I think that only gods could bear to look at that pattern. It is well that men cannot."

That was the morning when young Pryderi of the South came in with the men of Dyved. Joyfully he came, his white teeth shining in a fighting grin beneath his jewel-blue eyes and golden hair, his nose sniffing the air like a young, high-hearted hound's, eager for the chase.

"Greetings, Lords!" He came bounding up to the sons of Llyr. "Good be with you! And with the Lady, your sister. We will take off an Irish head for every blow that they have dealt her, and then we will open up that King Mouse-heart to see what queer kinds of insides he has got. Though by the Gods of both islands, I think somebody must have been beforehand with us and taken out his guts."

Then he saw by their faces how deep this went, beyond all grimness and all mockery, and his own face sobered, like a merry child's that suddenly feels pity.

"Indeed, and there would be no laughter with me either if the woman were Kigva, Gloyu Broad Realm's grandchild. Not until I had washed my hands in blood. I am sorry."

Bran smiled. "That lady has come to your house to sleep with you, has she not?"

"Three moons ago," said Pryderi proudly. "My mourning time for my father is over and I am king now, so I thought it was time I got my woman. And indeed, since I got Kigva," here his eyes danced, and a dimple in the left side of his grin danced with them, "I have wished for nothing except that I had got her sooner. It is a pity to have wasted so much time."

Bran chuckled. "Well, I see now that we owe you even more thanks than I thought for having come so soon."

Pryderi tossed his yellow head. "I am not wont to be slow on my way to battle, and if I had been this time it is not in the arms of that redhead that I would be lying. More likely the toe of her boot would be helping me forward."

"The women of her kin are warriors, are they not?" said Manawyddan. "Witch-priestesses of the tribes who dwell beside the Severn?" He thought, *I hope that Kigva has not got their temper; it would make her an ill housemate for Rhiannon of the Birds.*

"That is true, king's brother. I do not think any man ever lost his head over any of Kigva's aunts except when she took it off his shoulders." He grinned. "Nine of them, all old witches, and not a one but has a face that would scare a man away, even in the middle of the night. It is from the other side of the family that Kigva gets her looks. If her aunts could do her kind of witching, maybe they would not have taken up head-slicing."

Their ugliness may have been one reason why the Nine had become warriors, yet there must have been another. To keep the lands and the freedom that had been their foremothers' and that peaceful priestesses could hold no longer, they had taken war, their enemy, for their servant, and he had become their master. Was transforming, through them, even the face that their Goddess showed upon earth; so many are the traps set by change, the inexorable.

But what made them as they were Pryderi never stopped to think. Indeed, he seldom seems to have stopped to think, which is a little surprising, considering the blood that was probably in him. Perhaps he was too in love with life, too busy enjoying every breath of it, to stop for anything but sleep.

So at least, in the days that followed, Manawyddan read him. He loved to watch that zest, that young eager strength. Yet sometimes thought, never far from him, would come and lay a cold hand on his shoulder.

Risks enough at best, even for the young and swift and bold. But if Matholuch should use the Cauldron . . .

That would mean war such as the world had never seen. Extermination for the men of both islands, and the earth covered with savage speechless demons.

No man would risk that. Yet when panic drives a coward . . .

Manawyddan may have been glad that he had little time to think.

Like ants driven from their hills, men milled in that camp below Harlech. Ships were being built, weapons smithied. All eyes turned toward the sea, toward that gray road of waters that led to their goal.

Soon we shall be there! Soon we shall teach them! It is their whole heads we will have for a face-price, those dogs.

Many were grimly happy. Evnissyen was happiest of all. He thought proudly, *This is all my doing. Except for me there would still be peace. Bran would still be fooled.*

He could have hugged himself for joy in his own cleverness, pride in his own farsightedness. He never had been fooled by the outlanders' smooth, lying tongues.

Some men shared his own view of his shrewdness; for the first time he had a following. Foremost among his new admirers were Keli and Kueli, those sons whom Kymideu Kymeinvoll had borne within her womb when she broke out of the Iron House. Save for the ugly fire-red mark that twisted one side of his face no man could have told Keli from Kueli, and in their hatred of the Irish both burned with one flame.

"Our parents and our brothers trusted in their promises; in peace and in friendship they went into the Iron House. We know them, those outlanders who burned our brothers." Keli's eyes burned hotter than the brand upon his face.

"You can trust no promise they give, no oath they take. Every man, woman and child of that blood should die. Else all will be to do over again." That was Kueli, his eyes as fierce.

"So long as one of them walks the earth treachery will be breeding. No man of another race can walk without fear of a knife in his back, no child rest safe in its mother's arms or womb." Keli's blazing eyes had widened; his voice had risen to a grim chant.

They praised Evnissyen's discernment until he purred like a cat. He drank in every word; both their praise and their savagery went to his head like wine.

8

The Sinking Lands

The reason why so many ships had to be built was that they were not ships at all, but rafts and canoes, such as could sail in shallow water. Sails they had, but little else of true ships. The fleet could not take its natural road through the deep, because Bran was too big to get aboard a ship.

He might not have been able to get to Ireland at all had it not been for the Sinking Lands.

Many of them were gone already, those "lost lands" of Wales. The sea covered the tall forest that once had made the shores of Carnarvon one with those of Anglesey,* that sunken forest in which, in later ages, have been found not only the bones of the great bear and the red deer, but also those of oxen, the ancient servants of men.

The lands between Anglesey and the shores to the south were sinking, but not yet sunken. Trees still rose here and there through their muddy waters, giants defy-

*Sir William Boyd Dawkins.

ing the flood that had doomed them; fish swam through their lower branches and seaweed grew thick and rank where once fields had waved their plumes of golden grain. No beasts were there, and no birds but the white screaming gulls. All that water was salt, and no land thing could live in those lands, but left them to their lonely death. Like the Corpse God's own dominion they stretched there, a waste of sullen dirty waters.

Bran would have to walk through them, and his men dreaded that. But he laughed at their fears.

"Most of the time my chin will be above water, and when it is not I can swim."

"It is an unpleasant walk you will have," said Pryderi. "I would hate to wade through all that mud." He looked at it and shuddered; for once his gaiety was quenched.

"Maybe," said Bran, "but Branwen is having to bear far worse things than getting her feet wet."

"That is true," said Manawyddan, and pain crossed his face like a black wing.

"But do you be careful," he added. "You cannot see your footing through the darkness of these waters, and the ground is treacherous. If you sink, we in the ships will come close and try to pull you out, but I cannot say what will happen."

"I can." Bran smiled his big, good-natured smile that was the widest in the world. "The ships will overturn, and you will all get a mud bath."

"So long as that is the worst of it," said Manawyddan.

Frowning, he looked out across that hostile waste, that wilderness where the peace of death had not yet come, but only the ugliness and pain of a huge, once fruitful body in its death throes, hating to give up the warmth and goodness of the past. And he thought, *With how many of us will that be so before we come*

this way again? . . . Well, death too is a part of the
Great Going-Forward.

Naked, Bran waded down into the Sinking Lands,
save for the ropes that Manawyddan insisted should
be put upon him. They bound him to the ships that
kept as near him as they could, and he walked as close
as he could to the boundary of the Sinking Lands, to
the edge of the true sea. But in that too was danger.
It brought him nearer to treacherous drops, to the
edges of unseen cliffs.

Sometimes there was firm ground beneath his feet,
and sometimes the squashy softness of wet sand, and
over that he went as quickly and lightly as he could.
Bran could run lightly, for all his bulk.

Again he felt hard rock under his feet, and there
he went slow and carefully, guarding against a fall
from unseen heights. And then again the thick mud
squashed and belched under him, like some monster
of the Underworld spitting under his heel; and he
put on fresh speed because that mud sucked at him like
lips, it pulled at the sinews of his mighty legs with
might that made even him atom-small, with the strength
of forces that dwell forever in darkness and have no
gift or power but destruction.

Then he fell and, like arms, that sucking death closed
round and over him, like jaws whose teeth were the
more terrible for their softness, annihilation blacker than
night.

But out of those clinging depths great Bran surged
up, fighting, writhing, every muscle pulling, with heart-
tearing effort, against that black, enveloping embrace,
every toe groping, like a separate being, for foothold,
solidity, safety. Yet remembering, even in his agony, as
the harpooned mother whale remembers not to let her
threshing flukes strike her young in her death throes, so

Bran remembered not to pull upon those ropes that bound him to the frail barques that bore his men.

Then the groping toes of one threshing foot found and lost what they sought; brushed, for a breath's space, solidity. Fiercely he scrabbled back—thought it lost—found it again. His toes closed; through the clutching mud the other foot fought its way forward. With set teeth, his mouth and nose filled with muddy death, he braced himself for one last tremendous effort; the force of it seemed to snap his straining muscles, to split his whole being.

His head broke water. Above him he heard the shouts of frightened men. His mud-plastered eyes would not open, yet freed from that depth and extremity of darkness, their own smeared, blackened lids seemed like very light, clear and bright as the sky that once more looked down upon him.

He staggered on, and Nissyen, the lightest of his brothers, swam out to him and bathed his face, and brought him wine to drink.

He laughed then, looking up at the sun that he never had thought to see again; and from the ships his men applauded, and Manawyddan, still white and unsmiling, drew a deep breath of relief.

Beside him, Pryderi laughed. "It would take more than mud to kill Bran the Blessed!"

But for once Manawyddan spoke sternly to the young King of Dyved. "Be still, boy! You have seen a victory greater than any that ever will be won in Ireland, and one that was dearly bought."

Yet in truth no man had seen it, that battle fought in the darkness underwater, in the deeper darkness of that corrupted and envenomed earth, against that death like a mountain-huge, devouring tongue. Alone and unseen Bran had fought it and won it, and that no other man ever born could have done.

He plodded on, and the day wore. Sunset came. The pale shores of the Island of the Mighty had sunk into the gray arms of distance, and the white cliffs had darkened. The sky flamed like a mighty funeral pyre.

From the shores they had left, those ships looked small now, such toys as a child may launch on still pools or small streams while nurse or mother keeps guard. Bran's great figure, plodding through that treacherous waste, had shrunk to the size of a common man; had looked little and lost and wholly human, there in the vast graying loneliness.

It had dwindled to doll's size; then vanished altogether.

From the heights of those forsaken cliffs four men had watched it as long as they could: the sons of Beli.

When they could no longer see anything but the sails of the ships, Caswallon stirred. "I wonder what happened that time he fell. He was so slow in getting up that for a breath's space I wondered—but the blessing is still with him."

Lludd his brother sighed. "He will get to Ireland. Some of us should have gone with him. In my heart I knew that always. I hope he gets Branwen back safely. They say those Irish prize no trophy so much as a woman's head upon a pole."

"Because of the trouble the women of the Old Tribes gave them; they fought hard for the old ways." Caswallon shrugged. "Also it was Bran who sent her to Ireland, not we. And he cheated when he did, for he knew well that the Irish wanted her so that presently an Irish-born man might sit upon the throne of Beli. And all the time he meant that seat for Caradoc."

"Then his was the first wrong!" young Eveyd cried eagerly; he was the fourth brother. But Lludd and Llevelys, his elders, were silent, and presently Caswallon turned and looked at Lludd.

"You are the first-born," he said. "If you wish to claim your right I will support you."

Lludd looked back at him. "What right, Caswallon? The word has two meanings. Bran has been a good lord to the Island of the Mighty, and it is not I that will tear it, like a dog fighting over a bone, if Caradoc should reign after him. He would be a murderer that broke the peace and shed blood so, all for his own profit. While the land is happy, under Bran or Caradoc or another, disturb it not!"

"Why should that whelp of Bran's sit in the high seat after him, if we could not sit there after Beli?" Caswallon's laugh was like the tearing of silk. "It is we that have first right, and it is not I that will give that up! And since it is my right to be king, all people who do right must back me, and I will kill only those who do not, and so do wrong. The killing of wrongdoers is lawful."

"I have loved and dreamed of that kingship too long to defile it so," said Lludd. "A king is the servant of the people; it would be queer to kill some of them in order to get to serve all of them, and not so do I understand kingship."

"Then you will stand aside," said Caswallon.

"And what if Bran comes back?" said Llevelys. "He probably will; that Irishman is no match for him. Do you think the people will stand with you against him? I do not."

"There are many chances in war," said Caswallon. "It is in my heart that it is my destiny to be king."

"And would you kill Caradoc?" said Llevelys coldly. "You would have to, to sit safely on the throne, and that would be such a deed as is seldom heard of. Such as only the outcasts and outlaws have committed, they who walk accursed forever, to whom none may give food or drink or shelter."

"He is Bran's son, not Branwen's. No kin of ours . . ."

"He is our kin if we are Beli's kin. He is our cousin's son, our own blood."

Caswallon was silent awhile, then he said, "I have thought of that. Many people may think as you do, though indeed now the degrees and bonds of kinship will have to be reckoned in new ways; there will be much for a new king to do. And I will be that king. Bran has held our rights long enough; him I never could dethrone, but Caradoc I can. Him I will not stomach. But I will try to leave him alive."

Manawyddan looked back toward the island they had left behind. Back at the cliffs that now were a blur and a gloom, as though oncoming night already rested there. A black shrouding shape, she seemed to have settled upon the Island of the Mighty, like some huge bird upon her nest.

What eggs are hatching there? he wondered. But only the silence of the night answered him, the little whisper of the waters, the dull unhuman crying of the wind. And Bran trudged on through the Sinking Lands, steady, inexorable, as a mountain in motion, as one of the hills moving from their age-old places. So he went forward, blind as rock and earth, through the world that his movement already had shaken from its age-old foundations.

Herdsmen saw strange sights on the sea, and the word was borne to Matholuch.

"Lord, Lord, there is a forest rising out of the Sinking Lands—there where since our fathers' fathers' fathers' time nothing has grown at all—and it is moving! It is coming toward us!"

Matholuch called for his druids. "Use your sight," he

bade them, "and tell me what it truly is that these fellows think they have seen."

They said, "Lord, such journeys of the mind take time and preparation." But he would give them no time.

He would give them no time, so they closed their eyes and their lips moved soundlessly. Then for a few breath's space they were silent. Then all their mouths opened at once and they said, "Wood—wood—yes, they are wood. Many, many of them and tall—a multitude of them, and all moving . . ."

"But is it a wood?" demanded Matholuch.

"Something walks beside them, Lord. One, beside the many—something taller than a man, not so tall as a forest tree . . ."

"What is it?" Matholuch leant forward in his carved, gold-ornamented chair, his hands grasping the arms so that his knuckles showed white.

"Lord, it is moving . . . Twin brightnesses gleam near its top. Like water they gleam, but red . . . It is moving, Lord! Everything is moving! Toward the land. Toward all of us!"

They opened their eyes and shivered.

Matholuch sat like stone. His hands still clenched the arms of his chair, and his face was as white as his knuckles. He must have known: forests do not rise out of the sea, and only one reason could take ships into or so near the Sinking Lands.

Only one man could wade those shallows . . .

All there must have known, but with all their might they pushed the knowledge back, slammed and bolted the doors of their minds against it. *Let us not face it— let it go away—let it not be . . .*

But it was there. With every breath they drew it was drawing nearer. They all knew that; the King knew it. He licked his lips, and spoke at last.

"Well," he said, "well." And stopped. Then, "Nobody can know what this means unless Branwen knows. Ask her."

He did not offer to go to her himself.

They went, the nobles and the druids. They lifted the heavy spit off her and her out of the pit. They told her the tale, and it lost nothing in the telling.

". . . And beside the forest is a great mountain, and it moving. And near the top of the mountain are two bright shining lakes . . . Lady, what do you think this is?"

Indeed, they saw less Bran's body than his mind, and the wrath that overhung all of them like an avalanche.

Branwen's eyes shone; a faint, hard smile played round her mouth. "I am no Lady, but I can tell you what this is. The men of the Island of the Mighty are coming here, for they have heard how I am punished and dishonored."

Not a man there but had laughed to see her lowered into the pit. Not one of them all but now suddenly fell in love with his own feet; stared down at his shoes, as if trying to see through them, down into the wrigglesome and delectable and fascinating mysteries of his toes.

But they still hoped against hope. Naturally she would want to think that her people were coming, but it might be something else—it might be . . .

"Then, Lady," they asked politely, "what is that wood?"

"The masts of the ships," she answered. "As thick as a forest, the ships that bring the host from the Island of the Mighty."

They shuddered, and looked up toward heaven, but the ceiling was in the way, and it may have seemed to them that Bran was almost as depressingly near.

"Lady," they asked still more politely, "what is that mountain?"

She bloomed like a rose. Her face, that for so long had been wan and white save when the cooking fire or the butcher's palm reddened it, shone like the dawn.

"That is my brother, Bran the Blessed, wading through the shallows."

Bran, whom no ship could carry! They shuddered, but they tried once more. "Lady, what are those two lakes?"

"His two eyes, looking toward this island. The King is wroth, thinking how I have been treated here."

They left her then; they went back to Matholuch. They were eager now to let him have that leadership of which they had once deprived him, eager to let him be the head of the dog, not its tail. Like frightened children, they hoped that he could think of something to do.

But he railed at them. "This is all your doing! I never wanted to drive my wife from my bed, and insult her mighty kin. You are my councilors, and a fine job you have made of it! Now think of some way to undo what you have done, or I will take all your heads off. Surely they will be as much use off as they ever have been on."

They said nothing. Their silent faces were the mirror of his own despair. He raged at it and them.

"Speak! You did enough talking once. What emptinesses you have got on top of your shoulders! Lugaid, my love . . ."

He turned to his champion, that armed, bold hero whose like always stood near an Irish High King. Most likely Matholuch kept a regiment of them; he would not have wanted any ambitious man to get near enough to him to take his life and so his crown, as was the bloody way of the New Tribes.

But his chief druid got a little courage at last. No doubt he remembered Amergin.

"Lord, maybe it would have been better for all of us if you had given that order three years ago. But now it is too late. The deed is done, and you need all the men you have."

Matholuch remembered that forest of masts. The rage went out of him, and he sank back into his chair.

"Have we no hope at all?" he said weakly.

"We have Branwen," said the druid.

"Fool! All of you said that, three years ago."

"And the use we made of it was folly. But it is still true."

"Fool! Would you provoke him further? He must have a hundred men for every one that I can get together here before he strikes, and if I could win time it would help him, not me. In the north there are still many men of the Old Tribes, and they would rise to him, both to save their own skins and to take vengeance upon us."

"That too is true, Lord. We cannot keep Bran from avenging her. But the men of the Old Tribes hold their women dear. He may want her back safe and sound even more than he wants a face-price."

"I do not like your plan," said Matholuch, "but I will hear it."

"First, take her back to the House of Women," said the druid. "To her own Sunny Chamber. Send ladies to wait upon her there. Then let us prepare messages to send to him."

The men of the Island of the Mighty came ashore. They beached their ships near the mouth of the River Boyne, that sweet stream that is named for an ancient Goddess, the mother of Angus of the Birds. Not many miles from Tara of the Kings it flows, and past the Brug na Boinne, that splendid stone tomb that may be older than the oldest of Egypt's pyramids; it cannot be much younger. One thing is certain: not for Matholuch or the likes of Matholuch was it built.

Bran bathed there, in the Boyne. He washed off the mud of the Sinking Lands, and he got a hot meal at last, and a good sleep. His men feasted and rested too, but not all of them slept at once. The host kept a close watch.

The messengers came while Bran still slept. Manawyddan gave them food and drink. "When the King wakes you shall speak with him."

"Why waste good food and wine on the dogs, brother?" demanded Evnissyen. He took good care that they should hear him.

"Because, although they do not know the treatment that is due to women, we know the treatment that is due to heralds," said Manawyddan. "We are men. If a dog bites us, we do not bite him back. We have our swords."

"Although it is not on heralds that we use them," he added, seeing that Matholuch's men still looked unhappy.

Evnissyen flounced off, and Pryderi looked after him thoughtfully. "There are dogs and dogs," he said. "And a mad dog must bite somewhere."

The he bit his lip and looked at Manawyddan. "I forgot that he was your kin. Indeed, Lord, it is hard to remember."

Manawyddan smiled. "Only those who have madness in them need go mad because of any bite," he said.

Matholuch's messengers ate in peace, or in such peace as their own hearts would give them. They had hardly finished before they were brought to Bran. Even in his sleep he may have felt their coming; he whose heart was set now unalterably, sleeping or waking, upon one thing: one person's freedom and peace.

They looked at him, those messengers, and thought with relief, He is human, after all. A man like others.

Then they looked again, and thought, less comfortably, But he is very big. And something in his face awed them more than his bigness.

"Hail to you, Lord," they said, "and good be with you. We bring greetings from Matholuch the High King your kinsman. And from his noble lady Queen Branwen, your sister."

Bran thanked them, then said, "Have you word or token from Branwen the Queen?"

The messengers hesitated; they looked at the ground. But then they remembered their training; they stiffened themselves and faced him, like men going into battle.

"Lord, the Queen is safe in her Sunny Chamber, and there is nobody in Ireland who is not sorry that she was ever out of it. Nobody who would wish harm to a hair of her head, but . . ."

They stopped. Under Bran's eyes the words died. Their own eyes darted about like frightened flies, from sky to earth and side to side, and back again. They lit everywhere but on his face. They did everything but buzz.

"Would you threaten her?" said Bran; and his great voice was like a bear's growl deep in his throat. It was like a wind from angry heaven, a wind with power to sweep all things before it, and it blew Matholuch's messages away.

9

The One Vice of Bran

The messengers knelt before Matholuch; they told their story, and their voices ceased and died away.

Silence came then; silence that seemed to seep out of the council chamber through every nook and corner of Tara. The silence of the grave, or of a room in which a man lies murdered, of a place where life has made a sudden and more than usually unwilling end. Men heard their own breathing, and it was a mere thread plucked loose from the great cloak of that silence.

Matholuch lay back in his splendid chair and thought of what was to come.

He did not feel ready to face it. He felt queer and cold and sick inside. He felt empty; hollow where he should have been solid. His whole self was only a crust over hollowness.

He looked around at his men, but they too looked hollow; masks that his clutching fingers might twitch off to find empty air behind them. Nowhere the warm solidity of loyal hearts, loyal brains, loyal arms, to scheme and fight for him.

They were committing treason—they were not seeing him. They were seeing only themselves, their own fears, their own danger.

He was alone.

He tried to cry across the barriers, more terrible than any walls or any space, that separated him from them.

"You have undone me. You have betrayed me again. You have thrown away whatever chance I had."

But what chance had he had?

He moistened his lips and moistened them again before he could speak.

"Men, what is your counsel?"

"Lord," the eldest druid said, "there is only one counsel: you must give up the kingship to Gwern, your son. That may be a face-price that will satisfy even Bran, for it will break the laws of Ireland and make his heir our king. And it will save Ireland, for then we will not have a foreign prince over us."

And Matholuch bowed his head.

Messengers came again to the banks of the Boyne. Excuses buzzed around them like a swarm of bees.

"For nothing that was done with his good will has your kinsman Matholuch ever deserved anything but good of you, Lord. Indeed and indeed, that is so."

"Indeed, it is not much good that his good will is then," said Bran.

Pryderi put his hands on his hips and laughed. His white teeth shone scornfully.

"Indeed, if ever men of mine tried to deal so with my woman, it is fewer of them and none of myself there would be before they got it done."

The messengers were careful not to hear this. They said politely to Bran's feet, and not to his eyes, "All

that he can do he is doing, Lord. For the shame that
was put upon you and upon the Queen, by his own
people but not by his own will, he is ready to step
down from the high seat and give up all that he has.
To Gwern your sister's son he yields it. So shall the
heir of the Isle of the Mighty be High King in Ireland,
and Matholuch the Throneless shall be maintained here
or in the Island of the Mighty, or wherever you please."

Many stared in wonder. Light leapt into Manawyddan's face and into Nissyen's. But black fury twisted
Evnissyen's, and his hand flew to his sword hilt. The
men around him looked downcast and disappointed.

Their thought beat through the silence. *Have we
come all this way to be bought off with lands and
goods, when blood alone—seas of blood—can wash out
the insult?*

*And not even lands and good for ourselves, but for
the outlander's own whelp!*

Before they set forth on that hosting, not a man of
the Old Tribes would have given such a name to Branwen's son. But Evnissyen had sown seeds; war and
wrath had watered them.

Yet not even Evnissyen dared speak before the envoys were answered. Bran must answer them.

And Bran said nothing.

Like some great monstrous stone he sat there, like
the great Sun Stone itself where it still rears up, rugged
and gigantic, amid the stone circles of Britain's oldest
temple; it upon whose head each summer solstice still
brings the sun's self to rest, like a terrible blazing
crown.

He sat and said nothing, and Manawyddan's hand
tightened on the arm of the young King of Dyved beside him, until Pryderi gasped.

In Nissyen's face the light faded; as it faded in the
sky above. The day wore toward evening.

Still Bran brooded. He thought unhappily, *A good offer—a good offer—I wish it were not so good. It would save the Irish pride, and every man needs pride. It would give Branwen's boy what I want him to have. But I could not keep the little King of Ireland always with his mother and me in the Island of the Mighty; the Irish would have to have him part of the year— keeping him Irish, yet filling him always with this notion that he is heir to the Isle of the Mighty. While if he grows up in my court as a young landless prince, expecting to get Ireland at my death as Caradoc will get the Island of the Mighty . . .*

He opened his mouth, and then shrank from the thing that came out of it. So shatteringly loud it sounded in that stillness, and so much was shattered by it.

"Am I not to have the kingship myself then? When you offer me that, I may think about giving you peace. But from this time until that you will get none from me."

The men of the Island of the Mighty laughed loudly, for joy. The stricken faces of the Irish did not look too surprised; whatever they had hoped, those envoys of chiefs who had given little mercy can have expected little, knowing little of it. With folded arms and sad eyes Nissyen stared into the sunset, that now was making the sky bright again, making the west blaze like a burning world. Manawyddan's hand fell from Pryderi's arm, and his face was gray as death.

But Evnissyen laughed loudest of all, and the fires of the sunset glowed red in his dancing eyes.

"Now nothing shall stay our vengeance!"

They bore that word back to Tara. It brought night with it, black and complete. For here ended the hope of the Irish to keep their pride as a free nation. Here too were opened the red gates of butchery and slavery and rape.

That was a court of white faces and scared eyes and taut mouths. Every man went mantled in gloom, and every woman had in her eyes the dread of the sons of Llassar, whose brothers had shrieked and died in the Iron House.

Many of them must have marched with the sons of Llyr; be sitting by those distant campfires now. Eating Irish sheep and Irish cattle, as soon they would eat up all Ireland, crunching the green pleasant land in their mighty jaws.

They would be the most merciless of all, they whose stock had been merciless before they had anything to avenge.

The women who had been set to serve Branwen circled round her as though she had been a wolf. They told her nothing, and she asked them nothing. Speech had been scarce in the Sunny Chamber, since the first hour of the Queen's return; they had fawned on her then, but their ingratiating cluckings had died before the cold calm of her eyes. She thanked them for service done, as a Queen should, but unsmilingly. Now she saw that they suddenly seemed more afraid, and her heart leapt.

Can that mean that my brothers are drawing near? My brothers . . . !

Matholuch, the one man who had dreaded the making of peace, was the most frightened of all now that it had not been made. From the shadows his own face grinned at him, on its way back to the Island of the Mighty, on top of a pole.

He wondered if it would do any good to cut off the heads of his councilors—the heads that had spawned the cruelty and the insult—and send them in a kind of bouquet to Bran. In a last brief rush of rage he thought, *It is they that ought to die! They that have done it all!*

But he was not sure that any command of his would be obeyed now. They might well be plotting, those traitors, to send his own head to Bran . . .

He said at last, "Bring Branwen."

As a queen comes, she came to him. Like dawn rising after long dark night she came, beautiful as morning. Painted roses bloomed on her white cheeks, red satin hung about her, draped as though in flaming triumph those bones that would always be a poem, however age or drudgery might wither the flesh upon them. The noble thighs, the curved hips narrowing into invitation at the waist, the firm, sweet breasts like rare white apples; almost it seemed the same, that body that had been shaped to bear kings and be the lodestar of desire.

Matholuch put out his hands to her. It is likely that he never had loved her as he loved her then. "Branwen!" he cried. "Branwen!"

For to him the sight of her was morning. She was his one hope and his last chance. This was no ragged, accusing drudge from the kitchen, no stranger—she was his own, his Branwen. His wife, who had loved him. Surely she must still be enough herself to save him, to beg his life from her brothers.

But she looked at him, and his hands fell.

"Lord," she said, "what do you want of me?"

"Branwen." He could only stammer her name again. "Branwen."

"Speak," she said. "I still have one ear to hear you with." And she touched the still delicate-looking shell that could not. "For one thing I must give you thanks: that all these years your butcher has always struck the same side of my head."

"Branwen," he said, and his hands shook, "it was

not my fault. I never meant it to come to this. I sat there wondering what to do, and then you came and had no faith in me. You were angry, and I grew angry too . . ."

Again she looked at him, and he was silent.

She went on looking at him, and her face was like a carved face, that can neither be warmed by triumph, nor softened by pity.

She remembered many things, and she understood him now. Never would he have fought for her. That first time he had turned from her, in her own island, he had hated to leave her; as a hungry dog hates to leave a bone. He had had no thought at all, let alone pity, for her grief at losing him. After she had hurt his vanity, here in this same room, three years ago, he had tried only to forget her, not out of guilt or hurt love, but only out of hurt pride. Now he yearned for her again, as a scared child yearns for the warmth of its mother.

He drew courage from her silence. In her place he would have railed at his betrayer. If only he could get her into his arms, wake her passion again . . .

"Branwen—!" His voice was thick with a desire that she remembered well; one that brought back many other nights.

A stride had brought him to her, his hands were outstretched to grasp her, but she crossed hers upon her lovely breasts. They showed callused and chapped and ugly, rough against the shining silk.

One of them was blistered, and the nails of her long, tapering fingers were broken. Above their ruin her eyes shone cold as the ice of high mountaintops, ice that shall never melt till the world's end.

The King's hands fell again.

She said, "Call your councilors, Matholuch. We have nothing to say that should be said alone."

He sent for them, then waited, fidgeting, trying to

avert his eyes from her face that yet drew them like a terrible magnet. So in its seeming blankness a stone face, or the dead moon's face, may seem secret with an awesome secrecy. Far more chilling is such a mask when it comes upon human flesh . . .

They came, those men by whose counsel she had suffered. They greeted her warily, and she looked at them with those cold, calm eyes.

"Tell me how matters stand between you and my brother, Lords."

The eldest druid cleared his throat. He cleared it twice.

"Lady, we have offered your brother this face-price—" and he told her what had happened.

"Lady, surely it would be pleasing to you to see your son High King, and you cannot wish to see his realm laid waste. Nor can you wish to see the blood of the men of Ireland spilled for your sake, when the blood of men of the Island of the Mighty must flow with it and, living, they that have insulted you must bow down to you and be the servants of your son. They, and their children after them."

Branwen stood thinking, and that carved face did not change, any more than the bleak peaks of mountains change. The men who watched it shivered and held their breaths.

She said at last, "You give better counsel, Lords, than you did once. The King my brother should have been the first to see its goodness—he must be angry indeed. Are you sure that you have told me all that was said to him?"

"We swear it, Lady, by our hands and by the Gods we swear by."

"Then what has happened that you have not told me? Is one of my other brothers dead?" Her unwavering eyes fixed them, many-layered darknesses.

"No, Lady. There has been no fighting yet. We have told you all that has happened, as it happened. By the sun and by the moon, by fire and water, earth and air, we swear it."

She said, puzzled, "It is not like Bran to want blood."

Matholuch said eagerly, "We could send him the butcher's head—or the whole butcher to kill in any way he likes."

Then the darkness of Branwen's eyes flashed lightnings. "It would be beneath my brother's dignity to kill a servant for obeying his master's orders. He will not take the butcher's head unless I ask him for it, and I will not!" Her eyes said plainly, *"Ask yourself whose head he is likeliest to want, Matholuch, you who could not be more dead to me with it off your shoulders than with it on!"* and Matholuch shrank.

Aloud she ended, "Yet must we think what to say to my brother. I would not have men of my own people shed their blood for me."

"Lady," said the eldest druid, "you know him. Unless you can give us counsel we have none."

She thought, she searched her memories as a woman searches in a bag of old garments, rummaging among all that is cheap and all that is dear; among high cherished moments and the small commonplaces that time and death may yet turn to treasures fabulously dear. Great happenings and little happenings, and here and there an incident all shining like a jewel in the glow of some ancient tenderness. Memories that she had treasured and polished like jewels many a time during the long nights of those years when memory had been her only comfort.

Like the sudden opening of a door into a lighted room it came at last, the one she sought and needed, and she smiled, thinking how childlike all men were, both her great angry brother, and these who cowered guiltily, like scared children, before the whip of his coming.

"He hated it," she said, and a little tender smile brought back the dimples to her mouth, "he hated it when he grew too big to get inside a house. He never complained—he is no complainer. He joked about it, but he hated it. I was very little then, but I remember; it is one of the first things I do remember. Build him a house."

The hope that had lit their faces died. "Lady, how could we build him a house if he himself cannot?"

"He is not so big as all that," said Branwen. "He could build himself a house if he were willing, as he puts it, to squander so much of the wealth of the men of the Island of the Mighty. Wealth that is needed for things the people need. But I need not tell you the drains that there always are upon even the wealthiest king's purse. Or that there is nothing your own people now need so much as his good will."

They knew that, though they may have been thinking more of themselves than of their people. But their faces remained grave.

"Lady, the building would take time. And will he give us time?"

"Try him," said Branwen. "Say also that you will put the kingship in his hands to deal with as he sees fit. Once he yields a little, he will yield all. He is like that, big in all things."

They bore that word to Bran, where he sat in the camp of the men of the Island of the Mighty.

He sat with a naked sword across his knees, a sword the length of a lad near manhood. The heralds saw it and shivered, thinking how far it would reach and how its great sweep would slice a man like cheese.

"We hope this face-price will please you, Lord."

Bran said, "This is a lie to get time with."

"If you will give us time, the house will stand, Lord. Already the trees are being cut to build it. And this is done by the counsel of the Lady Branwen your sister, who hopes that you will not lay waste this island with war. This island that, if you will it, will be her son's kingdom."

"Branwen—" said Bran softly. And the thought smote him, *She may want that. To see her son a king.*

But he thrust that thought from him. He told himself again how unwise it would be to make Gwern king. And these men were wily; he glared at them.

"How do I know what she said or did not say?" he thundered. "What words you are putting into her mouth?"

But it was Manawyddan who answered, and his eyes were as deep as the sea they were the color of, and as steady as the changeless stars.

"These words are Branwen's own, brother. The Irish never would have thought of building you a house— that is her thought. Remember when she was a little girl and cried at bedtime, because you must stay outside in the dark?"

Bran looked past him; his great face worked. Then, "She shall weep no more because of me," he said heavily. "I will take the face-price."

The faces of the Irish shone like sunlight. Many of the men of the Island of the Mighty looked like dogs from whom a bone has been snatched, but as many more looked glad.

Bran's own huge shoulders were slumped as if in defeat, but the faces of Manawyddan and Nissyen were all light. Manawyddan thought within himself, *You have won a greater victory now, brother, than when*

you strove against those sucking depths in the Sinking
Lands. The greatest you will ever win.

Then of a sudden he heard a strange and very evil
sound: the grinding of Evnissyen's teeth.

10

The Price of a Crown

Trees crashed and fell, giants that it had taken ages of sun and rain to rear fell prostrate on that brown earth from which they had sprung. Across the green plain of Tara men and horses dragged them, and down the dark shining rivers they floated, bound together into rafts.

Night and day smiths toiled at their anvils; hammers crashed and fires burned. Metals glowed and melted, became screens and panels of gold, or of bronze chased with gold. Night and day wood-carvers toiled, straining their eyes to make in haste the intricate lovely patterns that would make plain brown wood as fine as shining metal. Nobles' houses yielded up vessels of gold and silver, and jeweled cups of ivory; coverlets and cushions of silk and fur and embroidered linen. Tara itself was looted. Nothing was spared that could make splendid the House of Bran.

Where it rose we do not know, there is no record left; but somewhere between Tara and the sea seems likeliest; where great Bran himself could watch its building, Branwen beside him. She was with her brothers now, she had her own pavilion in their camp, as once before she had had it in Aberffraw, for her wedding.

Great joy had there been at her coming. For the first time in three years—save for that one night she had sped the starling on its way—Branwen had wept, seeing her brothers, and no shame had been on her that the Irish who had brought her saw her do it, they before whom she had been proud and tearless so long.

"Bran!" she said, "Bran." Then, "Manawyddan!" And Bran passed her like a doll from his great arms to their brother's, his own eyes wet, and when Manawyddan took her his gray eyes too had the wetness of the sea for once, as well as its color.

Nissyen came then. His eyes were dry, but full of a great soft light.

"Good be with you, sister," he said, as his arms circled her. "Now and always."

She laughed and clung to him. "Good always will be with me, Nissyen, brother, while you three are."

Then she bit her lip, for she saw Evnissyen behind him. She changed her words quickly. "While you four are, sons of my mother."

He embraced her; he never would have foregone anything that was his due, but his eyes were hurt and angry.

"I came as far and as fast as the others, sister, and I am the only one that never would have given you to that Irish hound to chew. But because I always knew him for a foe and treated him as one, you hold it against me. That is like a woman."

She answered, "Evnissyen, it was only that I did not see you, and my heart was so full of the three I did see that I could remember nothing else. You are my youngest brother, the last to come from our mother's womb before me. How could I not be glad of you?"

But he thought only how ungrateful she was to him, the only one who would have saved her. How, as always, he had been slighted and rebuffed.

He glowered and gloomed, but he always had, so Branwen was not troubled. Even Evnissyen's jealousy and evil temper seemed good, they had such a flavor of home.

Her heart sang so loudly in its joy that the whole world seemed good.

Sometimes, alone in the dark watches of the night, she may have remembered that other pavilion at Aberffraw, where her lover had lain beside her. But all that seemed long ago, farther off than her childhood, that her brothers' coming had brought warm and close. Almost she could have smiled, as a woman smiles when in her housecleaning she finds some old toy that as a child she had lost and wept for, and now sees as something worthless and tawdry, all its magic gone.

All that is gone, it is over. It does not matter any more. Not unless Gwern should be like him, and I will not let him be. He has my blood too.

Gwern! Her heart cried that name as a lost child cries for home, as a man lost in a desert place cries for water. He was her one lack, her longing for him was unassuageable.

But I must not be greedy, I who have so much now! I who for so long had nothing. It is only for a little while. As soon as the house is built they will bring him, their king, for the feast and the peacemaking. A king belongs first of all to his people; we must not tread their pride underfoot too much. I must remember that, I, his mother, must learn to love them for his sake.

Soon now, soon! His uncles will see him, and I will hold him in my arms again—Gwern, Gwern, my baby! My son, who will be king of two islands some day.

But she cared nothing for that kingship, save because he would be proud of it. All she wanted was himself; bigger now, of course, but still warm and round and laughing. Still small enough to be carried in her arms . . .

The sons of Llyr saw her longing. Bran said, "Should we not send for the little fellow at once, brother?"

Manawyddan said heavily, "You know why not. It is not good for a people to feel conquered; they need what signs and symbols of freedom they can keep. We are bearing hard upon them, as it is. Most of these Irish chiefs will be plucked to the bone."

Bran said, "I must gift my men to repay them for this hosting; they are getting neither plunder nor battle glory from it. And as for these Irish chiefs, never was plucking more richly earned. When I think what they did—these woman-beating dogs—I still could take all their heads off!"

But his anger stemmed from more than one cause now. Those lords who must give him "gifts" undoubtedly were wringing as many of those gifts as they could out of the little people, the tillers of the soil. The many were paying for the brutish folly of the few.

Later it will be different, he told himself. *When all is in my hands. Justice will be done between all men then, as it is done now in the Island of the Mighty. I will bring back the ways of the Old Tribes.*

He chafed because he must tolerate and profit by injustice, because he must humor these men he despised. Not for the first time a thought crept through his mind like an ugly, sluggish worm. *They are taking much for granted. I have not yet said that the boy is to be king.*

If Gwern were not a king, Caradoc's crown would be safer. If he were not—if he were not . . .

Manawyddan felt his brother's unease. He said, "If we had taken the heads off these dogs, we should also have had to bury some of our own men, brother. Where no road is good one can still be better than another, and you chose the better."

Bran fidgeted. "I still have many choices to make, brother. Nothing is settled yet."

Manawyddan glanced at him keenly. "Surely the greatest matters are. Though it will be a delicate matter arranging Gwern's household: one man of ours for every Irishman, and each of them a sober man that will not step on Irish toes—"

Bran laughed shortly. "A household of cats and dogs that would be, surely! Better to take the boy home with us. Then he can be with Branwen always, and no trouble about it."

Manawyddan opened his mouth and then closed it again. He said at last, slowly, "Then he will return as a stranger, an outlander. He will be hated and plotted against always. While if he stays here he will be Ireland's own; most folk will cleave to him, even though for years our task will be no easy one."

"It will not. That we can depend on." Bran laughed again, yet more shortly.

"Yet in his manhood Gwern can bring about such peace between New Tribes and Old as our own isle knows. Do we not owe the people of this island that much, Bran? The Old Tribes, our own kin? The many little folk upon whom we have brought fear and hardship because of the deeds of one pack of high-placed hounds?"

But Bran stood like a mountain wrapped in storm clouds, in gray sullen darkness charged with thunder and lightning. He was divided in his own mind; he no longer knew whether he was going to do what was best, or what he wanted to do. He only knew, with the terrible stabbing suddenness of a spear thrust, that the two might not be the same.

Through all the years of his kingship he had striven to labor only for the good of his people. But was that true now? And when had it ceased being true? He looked into Manawyddan's eyes, and then swiftly looked away again, for those steady gray eyes gave him answer. *When first you set love for Caradoc above love for our people.*

He could not bear that knowledge, and so he could not bear the sight of his brother. He turned on his heel and left him.

It is easier to shut light out than to let it in; easier to block up a hole in a wall, after some fashion at least, than to knock that hole in it. Carefully, painstakingly, Bran filled up the hole that had let in the light he did not want to see.

As a dog guards a bone, as a miser guards his treasure, so Bran brooded over and cherished his doubt.

What kind of man would Gwern be?

Surely it was only prudent to wait and see. A boy cannot hide his nature as a man can. In six or eight years, maybe in only four or five, it might be possible to tell whether Gwern was Branwen's true son. And the joy of having him with her would solace any hurt to her pride in his future.

But the Irish will never believe that you are waiting. There will be unrest here and plotting, and finally bloodshed.

Bran brooded, and Evnissyen and his friends took heart again. They swaggered and preened themselves, and behind his brothers' backs they bullied the Irish in little ways.

Yet fear is hope's twin, and they were like dogs under whose nose a bone is held, a bone that at any second may be snatched away. Evnissyen thought with sick fury, *Why did the Irish have to surrender? Why did Branwen have to make Bran sentimental, just when he seemed to be getting sense at last? And all for the sake of that outlander's whelp! Of that wolf cub who will grow into a wolf . . .*

And beside him were those other twins, the sons of Llassar.

Kueli said, "Will the King your brother let them build him another Iron House? Can you not stop him? You did before."

Keli's teeth shone like a hungry wolf's. "Let them try it! Some parents here may see their children burn."

Evnissyen started; his nostrils quivered, his eyes grew wide. *Yes, I could stop Bran again!* He knew how now; and that knowledge was both terror and dizzying delight. It was a dream—something he never really would do, yet something he could do. A deed no man would dare; yet from that hour it tugged at him, lured and tormented him; he was afraid, and to ease his own torment he taunted Nissyen.

"You were getting your hopes up again, brother, but you have failed. Never will Bran hand over this island to the traitor's whelp."

Nissyen said, "What will be will be. It shapes in the wombs of the Mothers."

Evnissyen thought, *But I can shape it! Wipe the smiles off all your faces. Show all of you, who have always thought that I did not matter, that I am stronger than all of you put together. Able to destroy whatever you can build.*

He felt Nissyen's keen eyes. To blind them he laughed. "An easy way out. Will I never be rid of your whining, fool?"

Nissyen smiled. "You can never escape me, any more than I can escape you. For we were one being once, and shall be again."

Evnissyen stared. "Now that is madness, even for

you! Two people more unlike than you and me cannot walk the earth."

He flung away, and Nissyen looked after him, still smiling. "In every man is something incorruptible, however low he sinks, however invisible his true self may become, to himself and others. But you do not understand that, brother. Time was when you still could hear my voice across the gulf, but now . . . Well, every man must undergo many lives and many births before he can cleanse himself of the darkness and return to that Light whence all light comes. What does time matter, time that also must end?"

Had Branwen been less busy she must have seen that trouble was on her brothers. But Bran's house was nearly built. She was there from morning to night now, planning, overseeing.

Once fear did strike her. She laid her hand on Manawyddan's arm. "Brother, are you keeping something from me? Have you and Bran heard some rumor? About Gwern . . .?"

He smiled. "None, little sister. Your son will soon be here."

That eased her; they walked on to the house together. She was eager for his opinion of this and that.

"I want it to be just what Bran will like. This is his house, the first he has ever had . . ."

"It seems to me that you also want it to be what Branwen will like." He smiled again.

She dimpled. "You always see everything, Manawyddan. But when you and Bran go back to the Island of the Mighty, Gwern and I will live in this house. When he is a man Tara must be his home, I know; but never again can it be mine."

He looked down into her face that had sobered, suddenly aged; the face of the woman he was beginning to know. The young, laughing sister he had known from her birth was gone again.

"Girl, it is not Matholuch . . .?"

"Not he. Not one thing, but all . . . In this house they have dug no pit for a woman to cook in, brother; I have seen to that. Queens know too little about what goes on in their palace kitchens; maybe it is a good thing that I had to learn that. When I die no woman in Ireland will be toiling in a hot pit with the cooking spit on her shoulders.* I will lay it on my son to see to that, if I cannot manage it before he is a man."

"We will make it part of the peace terms, if need be. Bran will not like your staying here, but I thought you would not be parted from the boy again." There was a grim note in his voice, yet pride also. "Few women would wish to stay here after what has happened, but you have a brave heart, girl."

"And kin who are good friends to me. I had one other friend." She looked up at him. "Where is my bird, Manawyddan? Bran told me that he had given her into your keeping, so I knew that she was safe. Yet I am ashamed not to have asked before."

"I gave her to one who keeps many birds, sister, but cages none."

She laughed. "So Rhiannon has her! Well, may my son grow as tall and fine as hers! You have a right to be proud of him, brother. I had hoped to see my starling again, but if she mates and nests in Dyved I will leave her in peace."

Then her mind swung back to the house; to all the preparations that must be made for the night when Bran first entered into it.

"It will be the greatest feast that either island ever

---

*In the seventh century St. Adamnan's mother actually did enjoin upon her son to bring this relief to Irish cooks, as well as to secure other rights to women.

has seen, brother. All our men, and all the chief men of Ireland; all the kings that pay homage to the High King at Tara. And this time they will pay it to my son. Could any woman be prouder than I shall be? Or ask a better revenge?" Suddenly she laughed. "What does all that matter? Gwern will be there. My Gwern!"

Her whole being was centered upon him now, with the terrible singleheartedness of the woman who has turned her back upon love, and knows that her first-born will be her last. Deep within Manawyddan something shivered, as if in great cold; he thought he knew why. He prayed within himself, *May no fresh sorrow come on you through him, sister! From us, your brothers.*

On a day the house was finished. On its right stood the men of the Island of the Mighty, on its left all the great men of Ireland, their folk about them. Matholuch the King stood there in his red cloak and golden crown, and in his heart was a bitterness that almost outweighed fear.

Evening was near. The sun streamed red-gold across the plain, soft as a woman's hair; but under the trees the shadows lengthened. Black and monstrous, they stretched out many arms, and dreadfully, from the bowels of approaching night, their mother. Toward the House of Bran they reached. Hill-high it stood there, proudly disdaining their dark tentacles, seeming to create about it its own small night.

Into either side of it were set double doors of bronze, inlaid with gold. The widest doors ever seen.

Beside Pryderi another high-born young man of Dyved eyed them uneasily. "I wish we had not had to give up our arms, Lord."

"The Irish have given up theirs too," said Pryderi. "Under Queen Branwen's own eye the servants and ladies of Ireland are hanging up each man's arms above what will be his place at table. That takes time; it is why we must wait out here."

But he too felt uneasy. That vast pile, deep in its own black shadow, looked more like one of the mammoth tombs of the *Brug na Boinne* than the palace of a living king.

Then at last, and in the same breath's space, all four of those gigantic doors swung open.

Pryderi gasped; so did many men of both isles.

Huge indeed was that hall of Bran. Fire gleamed within its shadowy vastness, rose like red flowers from each of three great hearths set in the center of that great hall. A hundred pillars upbore the roof; a hundred tall trees that had been, stripped now of their green branches, encased in glowing gold.

All stood and stared; as if that hall that seemed too big for man were in truth the grand and aweful abiding place of a God; perilous for the feet of men.

Then Bran laughed his great laugh. "Come on, men."

Like the waves of the sea they surged in after him, and like another surging sea, through the doors upon the opposite side, swarmed the Irish, behind their gold-decked, bright-bearded shadow of a king.

So the men of two nations went into that hall that will be famed forever.

He did not go unhappily at the last, great Bran. While that house was being built he had thought of it with more annoyance than interest; it had seemed like a bribe and a trap. Long since he had ceased to miss the pleasant small shelter of houses; no roof can keep out the storms that beat upon a king. But now that it was here, that he was actually entering it, he felt boyish wonder and pleasure. He thought, *This is mine*.

The good smells of roasting meat and new-baked bread rose around him, brought a feeling of home.

On each side of each of the three hearths was a bed-place. Carved screens, glittering with gold, divided it from its fellows. There were set the couches where the children of Penardim and the King of the Irish would eat and sleep.

There Bran the Blessed met Matholuch; there warmth died, and cold courtesy took its place. Matholuch, drawing back to the other side of the great fires, the chiefs who had repudiated him around him, knew that there was no hope for him.

He will trust no pledge that I can give. He will neither let me stay here where I was born, nor go into exile in Gaul, where Gaulish chieftains might take up my cause. I must end my days a prisoner upon the Island of the Mighty.

And he thought of how he had first gone there in his pride, an army round him, to win the woman who now despised him. How different would this sailing be! Shame would pass; soon his main concern would be what comforts they would still allow him, what crumbs of splendor. Like a caged animal, in time he might learn to live only for the filling of his belly. But tonight his pride, or that vanity he called pride, writhed in white-hot anguish. All this pomp that surrounded him for the last time roused him to savage hunger, mocked him.

When he saw Branwen coming, beautiful as a bride, shining in all the splendor that became a queen, he turned away his head. Not in shame, but because she was one more thing of which he had been robbed. He did not look once at the small form that trotted beside her, the firelight catching in its red-gold curls—his pride once, now, perhaps, his supplanter . . .

She did not see him; she saw only her brothers. She led her son by the hand; before the sons of Llyr she halted, the noblest ladies of Ireland clustering behind her.

"This is Gwern," she said. Her eyes said, pitifully and proudly, *If I have shared a base man's bed, if I have been shamed and betrayed as no woman of the Island of the Mighty ever was before me, yet out of it all I have brought one good thing.*

The child was as fair as Matholuch, but his square little jaw, his nose, and the shape of his face, were Branwen's. And his eyes, blue beyond all doubting, not the almost-blue of Matholuch's, looked straight up into the eyes of his uncles. With an interested if somewhat awed curiosity.

The *Mabinogi* says that nobody looked at that child without loving him.

Manaywddan looked at him once, and then at Bran. He thought, while he prayed for it to be otherwise, *Now will we see how small the biggest man can be?*

Bran looked at the child and then at the mother, and deep within him something turned over. Something melted, and left him immeasurably relieved and immeasurably happy and immeasurably free. He caught up the boy in his mighty arms and tossed him toward the ceiling. His great voice boomed out so that the rafters shook.

"Hail to the King of the Irish! Hail to Gwern the High King! Let there be peace and brotherhood forever between my people and his!"

Then the Irish shouts too shook the rafters, and then Bran shouted again, and the men of both islands shouted with him.

In that whole vast hall all faces were stars of light save four: the grim faces of the twin sons of Llassar, the white face of Matholuch, the King that had been, and the death-white face of Evnissyen. The son of Eurosswydd stood there and ground his teeth. The cries of the outlanders' joy slashed him like whips, ran like poison through his veins.

But Bran beamed. He beamed sunnily, benificently, unbelievably; he looked upon everybody with eyes of love. He thought, *It is better this way. Better not to hold a nation prisoner until I die. Now Branwen will be happy. Both islands will have princes of their own blood and be happy, and build a sure road to peace. And Manawyddan will not be able to say anything.*

That last thought gave him great satisfaction too. He beamed a little more . . .

Branwen signed to the cupbearers and they brought drinking horns filled with rare wines. Bran sat down and called Branwen's son to him again. The boy came gladly. Children are not as fond of laps as most child lovers like to think, but here was one uncle who had a lap big enough to be comfortable. Gwern sat on it and approved of it.

From Bran he went to Manawyddan, whose lap was smaller, but not bad. Those sea-gray eyes were very friendly and warm and kind.

Then Nissyen the son of Eurosswydd called him.

This uncle was different. He was beautiful, as beautiful as Gwern's new-found mother, and as kind. His beauty seemed to flow out of him and make everything else beautiful, to find itself in all things and to fit all things into their places, and to show that those places were good. His very quietness made music.

Gwern could not have said any of those things, but he felt them. His eyes, that had been growing big and dark with excitement, grew soft. His head fell against Nissyen's shoulder; he slept.

Branwen found a moment to sit down beside Manawyddan. Her eyes too were soft.

"He was getting tired. I thought I should have to get

him away from all of you, but Nissyen knew. What is there that Nissyen does not know?"

Manawyddan smiled. "Another woman would have said, 'He should have children of his own.' You are wiser. Nissyen loves all living things; I think he sees into each so deeply, with such knowledge of its inmost self, that he loves it as no other can. But for him there is no love that binds him to one more than another; no love that shuts others out."

"You are wrong, brother. His love may know no bonds, but he is bound. To Evnissyen, as to none of us."

As if her words had been a wand to put his shape upon one of the shadows behind him, he was there. His eyes gleamed, restless as the leaping flames.

"Good be with you, my brother, my sister, noble children of Llyr. Surely it is, tonight. You have both got the stake you have played for." He moved forward, out into firelight.

The strange voice roused Gwern. He raised his head; the eyes that were as brilliantly blue as jay's feathers stared in wonder at the face that was like a mirrored image of the one above him. So like, yet so unlike . . .

Evnissyen smiled his wry smile. "First Bran, then Manawyddan, then you, Nissyen. All of you but me. Why does not my nephew, the only son of my sister, come to me? I would be glad to hold the boy, even if he were not King of the Irish."

Branwen sighed. "Gwern must go to him now, or he will be insulted again, and all of us will have put the child up to it."

Bran said, "Let the lad go to him, and welcome."

Gwern was used to being shown off. He rose and trotted obediently toward this new uncle.

Evnissyen sat down and dropped his hands between his knees, that none might see their frantic working.

With the madness of twisting, spitting snakes his fingers
writhed.

*Two breaths, three breaths, four—then I will have
him!*

The little feet reached him; stopped.

With a howl of triumph Evnissyen sprang. In one
lightning-swift movement he seized Branwen's son and
hurled the child headlong into the fire.

11

War

The little body hurtled through the flames and crashed through the burning logs like a club; his skull smashed like an eggshell.

One shriek the child had given, as Evnissyen seized him, a cry that changed horribly as the flames swallowed him. Branwen too had shrieked, and to Manawyddan, at her side, it seemed that that scream would ring in his ears forever.

Arrow-straight she leapt for the fire, but he sprang after her and flung her to one side. With his cloak thrown over his face to save his own eyes he bent and lifted that seared eyeless thing out of the fire. Branwen screamed again when she saw it, but its agony was over. Then Bran's great arm grasped her, and his shield covered her. From all sides the Irish, yelling with rage and horror, were leaping for their weapons. Their King had been killed before their eyes, and the war that Evnissyen had willed had come.

The men of the Island of the Mighty sprang for their

own weapons. Smitten shields roared like thunder;
swords and spears flashed. Men screamed as their flesh
was pierced. From place to place Evnissyen leapt and
slew, his face still aflame with unholy glee, and beside
him leapt and slew the sons of Llassar, Keli and Kueli,
their white teeth shining, their eyes red as the flames.
Nissyen kept his shield over Manawyddan, while the
son of Llyr fought the pain in his burned hands and
arms. Like a lion Bran raged before them, his huge
sword, longer than any other man's, clearing a circle
wide enough to keep all harm from Branwen, crushed
between his shoulder and his shield. Hampered as he
was, that whirling blade often helped or avenged his
men. That hall was like the home and birthplace of all
thunders, the crashing, shrieking core of all storms
that ever have battered the earth. The *Mabinogi* says
that no such uproar was ever heard beneath any other
roof, and in their far places the Gods Themselves may
have heard it, and shuddered at the power They had
given men.

Many were falling. Blood made the ground slippery,
and men tripped over bodies that lay forever feelingless
or that twisted and screamed again beneath that new
hurt. Friend trod on friend; the dead and the dying
were trampled beneath those milling feet.

Bran saw what was happening. His voice rang
through that tumult like the battle horns that shall blow
on the day of earth's ending. "Out! Out, men of Bran
the Blessed!"

He ploughed forward, through the press, his giant
sword whirling like a scythe before him, and all men
shrank from it. And all that were his own followed
him, hewing down those that barred their way.

Outside in the moonlit twilight he stopped and got
his breath, and the men of the Island of the Mighty
gathered round him. Manawyddan, his hands bandaged

in strips torn from his cloak, found that he still could handle sword and spear.

A breath's space, and the Irish were around them again, like dancing flames, and Matholuch came too, the center of an eager, swirling circle; he had seized his chance; however little they honored him, the Irish were used to following him, and they had nobody else.

He fought well; many a man of the Island of the Mighty fell before him that night, but he never pressed too close to that place where his mighty brother-in-law towered.

But for awhile that rush needed no stronger leader; frenzy begot it and frenzy fed it. And when vengeance was forgotten another madness took its place. They were no longer men who fought there; they were deaths, lowering dreadfully at one another. To himself each man was still flesh, but those who came at him were grinning at him through skulls, and clawing at him with the bony hand of extinction; and as he saw his fellows so they saw him. Each man rammed sword and spear into as many of those living threats as he could reach.

Dawn found them there, gray men fighting amid gray shadows; as perhaps every man who fights in war fights a shadow, the death that he sees as death because it sees him as death; so that out of their common passion for life all are turned into its foes and kill.

Dawn fell on their worn faces, and their fever left them. They shivered there in the harsh gray light.

The Irish retreated toward Tara, and Bran and his men went back into the house that had been built for him; the house that was to have sealed the peace.

Within that vast hall all was ruin; the fires out, the furniture smashed, the floor covered with blood and dead men, and with the moaning wounded.

They laid what had been Branwen's son upon the couch prepared for the King of the Irish; Branwen slept like one dead upon her own couch, and Nissyen sat beside her, those strangely magical hands of his near her head, where at need they could fetter her faster in sleep. Sometime during the slaughter she had fainted behind Bran's shield; and oblivion was the one good left for her. She slept . . .

Bran and Manawyddan did not sleep; they saw to the treating of the wounded, the carrying out of the dead. Food and wine were found; the preparing of a meal begun.

Before the relit fires Evnissyen and Keli tended each other's cuts; Kueli, who had taken a real wound, sat down. Evnissyen's eyes still danced; he had not yet noticed that all men but those two had drawn away from him.

He said, laughing, "Long will the Irish remember this night!"

Then he felt the eyes of his brothers upon him, the eyes of the sons of Llyr, and a great coldness came over him. The laughter faded from his face. But he gathered himself together again, and burst into quick, savage speech.

"Well, brothers, what have I done but the sensible thing? He was the traitor's whelp, and the bigger you let him grow the harder he would have bitten. Our sister made his flesh—fair flesh—but the seed it was shaped round would have rotted the heart out of it. You love peace, Bran—what peace could you have had while he lived? Would you have wanted his knife in Caradoc's back? Or, more likely, his poison in Caradoc's belly?"

Bran said slowly and grimly, "Speak not to me of Caradoc, Evnissyen, lest I remember what will be in my sister's heart when she awakes. What would be in mine if it had been Caradoc."

Manawyddan said as grimly, "Many men of the Island of the Mighty died last night for this sensible deed of yours, Evnissyen; this kin-murder. And many more will die."

Evnissyen cried out wildly, "It was not kin-murder —you cannot say that! I was careful not to shed his blood, I only put him in the fire . . ."

He stopped before Bran's face, that was bleak as wintry dawn on cliffs that frown, eternally relentless, above northern seas.

"Do not remind us that that is not shedding kindred blood," he said. "Do not speak of fire. It is not safe for you."

Evnissyen shuddered and for once was still. For awhile all men there were still.

Then Pryderi looked up from the sword he had been cleaning, and his eyes were as bright as the blade.

"Indeed," he said, "I am no kin at all to this son of Eurosswydd. If you would like him to die, Lords, I will be glad to go outside with him and persuade him to do it."

Evnissyen's teeth flashed like a wolf's; he was himself again. "When we get back to the Island of the Mighty and have no born foes to fight, I will make you answer for that, Pryderi, whom Pwyll was fool enough to call son!"

"You will get that answer," said Pryderi. "But why try to sneak out of asking for it now? It is ready I am to give it."

Bran said, "Let no man here shed blood of the Island of the Mighty. The Irish will do enough of that."

He turned his great back upon them, and again there was silence.

In that silence Evnissyen found that men looked away when he looked at them, and drew away when he neared them. He came at last to the doorway by which the twin sons of Llassar were sitting, fierce Keli and Kueli. He began to tell them how wise and farseeing he had been.

"That cub might have ground the whole Island of the Mighty under Ireland's heel. I stopped that; yet what thanks do I get?"

But then he stopped speaking, for he saw that nobody was listening to him. Kueli's wound was worse than he had thought, and Keli was busy with it, trouble on the side of his face that looked like other men's.

Evnissyen sat still and looked at no one, and knew that once more he was alone.

Only Nissyen, who sat by Branwen, looked at him, and his face was saddest of all.

The day wore. Bran had his dead burned and a great pit dug to bury their ashes in, and the old women of the Irish came and dragged away their dead.

Some of Bran's men grumbled, and said that they wished that the men of Ireland had come instead. A few laughed and said that the Irish cowards had got a bellyful soon. But most said nothing at all. They were beginning to wonder, *When will they come?* The man who can rejoice most savagely when he meets his foe face to face, still likes to know where that enemy is, and what he is doing.

They could see the hill of Tara; the ramparts that surrounded the place called the Seat, where kings had dwelt from of old. Since the morning of the Western World, when all kings reigned in accordance with the Ancient Harmonies.

Nothing moved on those heights; there was only sunlit silence.

The shadows grew blacker; the arms they stretched out over the plain grew longer and longer. Nothing happened.

The sun set, red and wrathful, in the west.

The men of the Island of the Mighty watched her go, and felt themselves grow colder. That was not strange, for autumn was upon them, and already the nights were chilly. They went inside, and ate and drank; they would have drunk too much, had the sons of Llyr let them. They sat round the fires, and piled the firewood high. Like angry snakes the red flames hissed. Branwen heard them where she lay and shuddered, covering her face; she could no longer bear the sight of fire. Nissyen stroked her hair gently, with his long, fine fingers.

There was a sudden stir at the door that faced Tara. One of the guards set there hurried to Bran.

"Lord—" he stammered, "Lord, there is something wrong with the moon. It—it is where it ought not to be."

"Where is it?" Bran's huge frame stiffened.

"Lord, it is too low." The man's lips worked. "Too low. It is not in the sky at all."

Bran rose and made for the doors. Pryderi would have followed him, but Manawyddan laid a hand on his arm.

"Best if we stay quietly where we are, lad. Where the men can see us. We want no panic."

Pryderi sat down again, though not happily. Bran reached the doorway alone.

Round and red it glowed there, upon the ramparts of Tara. A gleaming balefulness. A squat, strange witness to the mystery of shape, that can be shared by a child's ball and by the sun; by the tiny and by the infinite. The circle made solid; without end and without beginning, the very shape of eternity itself. Unalive, yet full of life; smoke rose from it like grim breath.

Bran looked, and his big face grew pale, and then paler, like a mountain whitening under winter snows.

"The Cauldron—the Cauldron . . ."

The cry was Kueli's. He was running, staggering as he ran, he who since noon had not been able to rise, and his face was blanched with horror.

"Come back! You must be still—" Keli his brother caught him. Other men swarmed after them.

"No, brother, no! We must flee. They will send the dead against us!"

Kueli fought to free himself, to reach the doors, and suddenly a red flood came pouring from his mouth. He gasped; his head fell forward, and he fell forward, against his brother's breast. His breath rattled, and he died.

Keli laid him down. He turned to face Bran, and the red mark on his face worked like a living thing.

"My brother spoke truth, Lord. Yonder is the Cauldron that my father and my mother stole from the Underworld—the Pair Dadeni, the Cauldron of Rebirth."

All gasped; all stared. Not a man there but knew of that Cauldron, in which memory must be drowned before each soul could rise from it to return to earth and find a new body in the warm womb of a new mother.

"Yes, they stole it," Keli's laugh was wild, "they, the only two since time began to break out of that world by force! *They* did not choose to lose their hard-won battle skills in its depths—they thought to set mankind free from the Gods forever, free to shape his own destiny."

"But how—?" Pryderi stared; he had come up with Manawyddan.

"How have the Gods managed without it, you mean?" Keli's laugh was still wilder. "Somehow They have, for there is still birth in the world. My mother herself was afraid for awhile; she told me once that she feared she might not be able to get souls for her own sons. Well, we soon shall know. They will slay us all, those demons that come out of the Cauldron now!"

"Be silent," said Bran harshly.

Keli swung back to him. "Woe on the day when my father Llassar gave It to you, against my mother's counsel, Bran no-more-the-Blessed! You that gave It to that Mouse-heart, to him who forsook your sister as he had forsaken us! Once traitor, always traitor, till the Cauldron has washed the soul times without number. Did the Mothers turn their backs on you, or the Gods make you mad, that you rushed like this upon your end?"

Bran said, "I am not yet ended. No man ever has been, and no man ever will be."

Yet again Keli laughed, and the scar that was no scar twisted like a crimson snake.

"Maybe, maybe not. No men before us ever have met their deaths by such hands as we shall die by. You that we called our friend, that should at least have been your own, you should have known better than to give the Cauldron into the hands of those that burned the children before the mother's eyes. I could have told you what these Irish were—I on whose face they set their mark while it was still within my mother's womb! Well, Kueli is dead now—the one of us two that women liked—and I thank the Gods, those foes of all my kin, that he died as other men die! A clean death, not such a one as you and I will know."

Laughing like a madman, he turned and fled into the night. Pryderi would have sprung after him, but this time it was Bran who laid a hand upon his arm.

"Let him go, boy." He turned to the men that crowded around them, clustering white faces already ghostlike, stiff with a fear that ghosts cannot know. "Let us get to bed now, men. Tomorrow we will need our strength."

In his vast quiet there was something quieting. It

soothed them all. One man even laughed, though that laugh was not steady on its legs.

"Here is one that they cannot raise again!" He held up a head that he had taken the night before. "Or if they can, it will be hard for him to see where to smite."

His comrades laughed uproariously, though there was a queer twitch in their laughter. But Manawyddan looked at the head and said thoughtfully, "Were I you, I would guard that well."

The man's face whitened a little. "I will," said he, and tied it firmly to his spear by the hair.

They lay down with their shields and swords beside them. They slept, and their souls went out of them, held to their bodies by those slender silver cords that but one knife can sever, that which is held in the hands of death, sleep's sister. They slept soundly; to know the worst is to find a kind of peace.

But in the last watches of the night, in that deep darkness that goes before the dawn, a great cry rose up and the sleepers woke. They snatched up sword and spear and looked about them for the foe, but whichever way they looked the darkness covered their eyes, the vast bodiless enemy that hemmed them in.

Until torches were lit, and they saw a man cowering and gibbering on the ground, past screaming now, but still pointing with his hand . . .

At a spear that was bounding over that ground before them, and as they looked, astounded, they saw what made the spear move. A head whose hair was tied to it was hopping swiftly, grotesquely, toward the doors. Its glazed eyes shone red and its bared teeth shone white.

All men gave a yell and sprang backward. Only Bran and Manawyddan sprang before the doorway, where the entranced guards stood staring at that head as birds stare at a snake.

Pryderi leapt forward and grasped the spear by the

haft, as far as might be from the head. But it spun round and sprang at him, somehow aiming the spear at his throat. That deadly lunge seemed sure to spit him; again all men cried out.

Light-swift, Pryderi twisted to escape the thrust, then yelled as the head itself jumped sidewise and fastened its teeth in his throat.

He tore it away and hurled it to the ground. For a breath's space it lay stunned, then sprang at him again. But this time he sidestepped, and drove at it with his own spear. Again and again it dodged and leapt, trying to reach him again, while he as vainly tried to spear it.

Bran and Manawyddan made the doors fast, and Bran set his great bulk against the nearest. Manawyddan turned to help Pryderi.

But in that instant Pryderi kicked at the head with his left foot, while it was watching the spear that drove at it from the right. That kick caught it and sent it bouncing into the embers of the fire, where it screamed like a man in agony. Pryderi leapt after it and stamped upon it; time after time he drove his spear into it, but still it sprang at him, howling with rage and pain.

Then Manawyddan brought him an axe, and with that he smashed its skull, though he had to smash it into little bits before the pieces stopped leaping at him.

When all was over the men rejoiced. They shook their spears and laughed. "So must we all do tomorrow! Cut off their heads and smash them! Then they will not rise again."

Pryderi sat down and rubbed grease on his scorched feet, and Manawyddan bathed his wounded neck. The son of Llyr used druid power on that wound, as Bran had on his burns, for there was no telling what poison might have lurked in those demon teeth.

But Branwen wept for what those screams had made her remember, and could not escape again into sleep.

Morning came, and with it the host of the Irish, and some had the faces of men, but most had foaming mouths that snarled and slavered and gnashed bared teeth, yet made no sound. Long and hard was that battle; many men died. Matholuch kept those demon-housing bodies always in front, so saving the living and wielding his deadliest metal, the Undead.

One by one those dead men fell, cut into too many pieces to rise again. Living Irishmen took their places, white-faced men who shrank from the devils they fought beside.

Bitter and long was that battle; it ended only with the day. Then the Irish went back to Tara, and the tired shrunken forces of the Island of the Mighty turned back to the House of Bran.

A man named Rhun turned aside to drink at a nearby stream; he was the man who had cut off the head that had fought with Pryderi. Night was falling, and he thought he heard a rustling behind him, but when he turned to see if one of his comrades was there, he caught only a glimpse of someone scuttling clumsily through the bushes; someone too short to be a man.

Is it an Irish child? he thought, He called after it, but only once, for he was very tired. He went on, down to the stream. He stooped to drink, and in that instant something pounced on his back, and long arms grasped his neck . . .

His comrades heard his scream, and came running. They found him lying there, his head twisted from his shoulders. A thing the like of which they never had seen before was dancing upon his body and brandishing his head. Its own body was a man's, but from its shoulders rose no head, only the red stem of a severed neck.

Screaming, they ran back to the House of Bran.

"Well," said Pryderi when he heard, "it has got Rhun's head in place of its own. It is me it will be wanting next. I will not keep it waiting."

He rose and rearmed himself and went down to the stream. His blue eyes and his sweet, gay young mouth were set and stern; for once all his smile was gone.

The thing could not have seen or heard him coming; it had neither eyes nor ears. Yet as he came within sight of the water it sprang.

He was ready. He sidestepped its spring and with a great slash of his sword cut it in two. Its legs fell one way and its arms the other. Yet in a flash those arms were reaching for his neck, and the legs were twining round his. He seemed to be fighting four foes at once, all of them quick and fierce as lightning. He had a hard fight before he got them all chopped into little bits.

But next day only dead men came against the men of the Island of the Mighty. With horror Bran's men recognized the faces of men they had killed not once, but twice; the cauldron had power to weld the smallest bits of flesh together again, into a whole man. And that night scouts brought word that more Irish were pouring in along the roads that led to Tara. The men of the Island of the Mighty were in hard case; they could hope for no reinforcements, and their dead did not rise.

"Once the Old Tribes might have helped us," said Manawyddan, "but not now. Not since they have heard how uncle burned nephew."

He looked at Bran. "Shall we try to reach the ships, brother?" The night was well worn, and the chiefs sat alone in council.

Nissyen raised dark eyes. "What of our wounded? Many of them could not walk so far."

With stern sorrow Manawyddan met those eyes. "Better to lose some lives than all, boy. And our sister is with us."

Bran said heavily, "We could never get there. What whole men we have left could not fight their way so far, with those demons free to come at them from every side. Here we at least have walls at our backs."

"Let us make a surprise attack," said Pryderi. "If we could capture the Cauldron—" His eyes sparkled.

"The ramparts of Tara were well planned," said Bran. "And the spot where the Cauldron sets is well chosen. Two of those devils could hold it against an army."

For a space there was silence. Then Manawyddan said at last, "There is only one thing left to try. To-morrow we must hold the Irishwomen, so that they cannot bear warning to Tara, and burn their dead along with ours. I doubt if even the Cauldron can raise men from ashes."

But next day at sunset when, after great carnage, the dead were burned, only one armload of Irish fragments was thrown onto the fire. Somehow its fellows knew and fled. Like an enormous pack of rats they scampered off toward Tara. Over the green turf they rolled and hopped and bounded, a grisly squirming mass. Weary and bleeding the men of the Island of the Mighty pursued them, but in vain. He who caught up with them was tripped and thrown, and in a breath's space the flesh was stripped from his bones, so fierce were the nails and teeth of those bodiless hands and feet and heads.

That night, for the first time, the doors of Bran's House were closed. Men huddled round the fires and tried not to think of the Cauldron glowing balefully, like a star of hell, upon the Ridge of Tara; of those shadows that even now must be squirming over its sides: the dead swinging back, with lithe and dreadful suppleness, into the world of men. Within that house was darkness far deeper than that of the night outside; long indeed it seemed to those within since they had set forth in their pride and strength to punish the outlanders, they who now waited like trapped beasts for the butcher.

Sleep came at last to seal their eyelids, to bear them to worlds that the waking brain is too coarse to remember.

When the darkness was deepest Nissyen woke. He heard stealthy movement near the doors, and softly he rose and crept toward it. His hand found another hand and touched it.

"Evnissyen," he said.

"You again!" The whisper was an angry hiss. "Would that I had slain you in our mother's womb! There at least there would have been no fools to cry 'Kin-murder!'"

Nissyen said, "What do you seek to do, brother?"

Evnissyen said, "I have not made up my mind yet. But something must be done."

They went out together, and closed the doors behind them. They walked over ground that would have been white with frost had there been light enough in the world for anything to be white. The moon had set and clouds veiled the stars, but upon the hill of Tara the Cauldron still glowed dully. No shadows moved round it now; for that night its work was done.

"He had a good notion, that loudmouthed pup of Manawyddan's," said Evnissyen, "As far as it went. To destroy the Cauldron would be easier than to capture it. If we could throw it down from the walls . . ."

"First we must reach it," said Nissyen. He thought,

*You play with straws because you cannot keep still.
Because you know in your heart that you have brought
death upon all our folk.*

"There must be a way."

For awhile they walked in silence toward Tara, then
Evnissyen laughed harshly.

"They say that this island breeds no snakes, yet it
has bred Matholuch. See what his snake's cunning has
brought us all to."

Nissyen was silent.

"Even you must have wit enough to see what game
he plays, brother. He looks to his living dead to kill
us all and to us to kill enough of them before we die
that the men of Ireland can handle them afterward.
Then he can sit in peace at Tara and smirk. Oh, he
is clever in his slimy way, the outland snake! If only
Bran had not been fool enough to give him the Cauldron . . ."

He screamed then, as a spear shot through the darkness and struck him in the leg.

They fled, but all around them the shadows were
coming alive. Flowering terribly and blackly into the
arms and shouting voices, into the running feet of men.
Arrows and more spears whizzed after them. Nissyen
half carried his brother, but even so Evnissyen stumbled
and staggered. And behind them a torch blazed into
red light.

"Quick, brother!" Nissyen's grasp tightened. "If these
are living men, they will know you for their king's
murderer . . ."

"Fool!" Evnissyen tore himself free. "You use that
word—of the scotching of a young snake . . ."

Then such pain took him that he fell, writhing.

There was a thicket beside them. Light-swift, Nissyen tore off his own green cloak and the flame-red one
that Evnissyen always wore. He pushed his brother

under the bushes and covered him with the green cloak.

"Lie still, brother. Even if they catch me. You can do nothing, and I do not want to die for nothing."

He ran, the red cloak whirling round him, and the torchlight found it and made it glow like new-shed blood. Shone as mercilessly upon the face that might have been Evnissyen's own . . .

The shout went up, fierce as a hungry beast's: *"Gwern's slayer!"*

More spears hissed; he fell. They closed around him and laughed with savage glee. They would have liked more time; they would have liked to carry him back to Tara, where Matholuch could have shared the vengeance. But the House of Bran was nearer, and from it already voices were coming, and the clank of arms.

They did not have time enough to deal with Nissyen as they would have liked, but they had time enough. They hurt him as much as they could.

12

The Slayer of Two Kings

Morning came, and with it the host of the Irish, and this time they carried Nissyen's head upon a pole. Cries of rage and grief went up from Bran's men when they saw it; like one man they hurled themselves upon the foe. The living Irish had to come to help the dead.

All day long that battle raged; sometimes it broke against the ramparts of Tara; sometimes it rolled back and broke like a wave upon the walls and doors of the House of Bran. Terribly it raged, like a fire that in time of drought seizes upon a forest and all the host of forest dwellers, and devours all, big and little, both the green trees and the winged and furred things that try to flee and cannot, so that at last only stumps are left, and bits of charred wood and bone.

The men of the Island of the Mighty took back Nissyen's head, but the life that had been in it they could not put back, and they paid for it with many of their own.

All through that battle Evnissyen lay beneath the

bushes; sometimes he heard it and sometimes he did not, for his mind flickered in and out of him as a dying candle flickers.

I could call them now, they would hear me and come . . .

But he knew that he would not; that he never wanted to hear the sound of any human voice again.

Why should I wish to rise again, when I could not rise while you were still alive, Nissyen? When they were tormenting you . . .

Again his mind left him. When he woke again night was near. He moved a little, beneath that green cloak that was the color of all growing things. He saw the sky above Tara, the white vastness of it turning slowly to darkness, and he saw the Cauldron beginning to glow dully; they had lit the fire beneath it. Soon they would begin to revive their dead.

And he thought, *Not even that Cauldron could bring back Nissyen's own sparkle to his eyes, or his laugh to his lips, or the softness of his voice. How little power there is in miracles, that this one could make Nissyen walk and fight again, if he were put in it, and yet never could bring him back.*

He had never wept except for rage; his eyes did not know how. He could only lie there and feel the pain seethe within him, burning like fire, tearing him like claws.

He is dead, and he died for me. Not because he thought it his duty, but because he cared what happened to me.

The only eyes that had ever met his warmly, unshrinking, unrepelled. The only one who had never had to try to be kind.

I am all alone now, forever . . .

The others had always tried to be kind. He had always known that, and hated them the more for it.

Because they had had to try. Why had everything always gone wrong? What had been the meaning of it all? He was too tired to think; also the eyes of the mind that belonged to his present body were not capable of seeing why.

He looked up and saw the Cauldron, red now as the sun that had set; red as a fallen star gleaming through the dusk of hell. Black smoke streamed from it, darkening the darkening sky.

Each day we kill them, but each day they rise again and kill more of us, and our dead do not rise. So it must go on until they kill us all, until they mow us down to the last man, as the reaper mows the grain. The host of the Island of the Mighty will be no more, and the outland cowards will take all our heads and laugh.

He told himself for the thousandth time, *It is Bran's fault, not mine. Bran gave away the Cauldron.*

But he was too weak to kindle the old fires, he who had always had so many fires of wrath to warm himself with. He was alone in the cold and the dark forever, and over the frozen wastes a voice howled, a voice that he could no longer shut out: *"It is your deeds that have brought the men of the Island of the Mighty to this. You hate the outlanders, and your hatred has given them this good gift: the conquest and destruction of your people."*

And within himself he reeled and gave the cry that erring humanity has given throughout the ages: *"I did not mean it! I did not know that it would be like this."* And the inexorable answered him, *"Yet so it is, and by your doing."*

He accepted that; and that was the first time in his life that Evnissyen ever had accepted responsibility for anything that went amiss.

He said, "O Gods, woe is me that I am the cause of this slaughter of the men of the Island of the Mighty, and shame be upon me if I do not seek their deliverance."

He lay very still, and out of his pain an idea was born, the far white shimmer of mountaintops upon it, as out of pain a child is born.

He threw aside the cloak, he pulled the spear from his leg. With blood and mud he smeared his face so that none could have known it. He rolled out from under the bushes; he kept rolling, painfully, until he came to a heap of the Irish dead.

They were two Irishmen without trousers, the *Mabinogi* says, who found him. They hoisted him onto their backs, grunting and groaning, "Here is a big one!" They were all mighty men, those sons of Penardim, men of beauty and power.

He did not have to pretend to be stiff. Upon that battlefield were many soulless, who still were soft and warm.

They carried him back to Tara, and up upon the ramparts. He felt a hot wind blowing upon him; it grew stronger.

The Cauldron . . .

They were lifting him higher; he knew why. The heat of its steam smote him. Fear took him, sudden fear of the boiling depths that were about to receive him.

Can I do what I meant to do? Can I do anything, in that agony?

I must do it.

Doll-limp—be doll-limp. You must not stiffen now; they must not guess that you breathe. Doll-limp; like Branwen's dolls that you used to break, you who now have broken her last and most precious doll of all . . .

Their hands were loosing him, falling away. *He* was

falling—down, down. He could do nothing but close his eyes.

O Gods, O Mothers. Agony indeed—hot, searing agony! Is this what Gwern felt?

Then, suddenly as it had come, it was gone. He still felt and smelled the heat and the fumes, the boiling bath of regeneration laved his whole body, but mysteriously it no longer burned. He had a feeling of vast spaces around him, of being outside the world, and yet deep within the world.

In the very womb of the universe . . .

He did not wait to see what it would have done to him. He stretched out his arms and legs as far as they would go. He stretched with all the might that was in him, and with all the violence and rage and fury with which he was gifted above all the sons of women.

He felt his sinews cracking, and then his bones. His lungs labored in fiery torment. He gasped for air, and let in burning heat; the pain came back. He lived through eons of struggle and torture, he stretched and pushed and strained when it seemed that he could not, by any power human or unhuman, stretch and strain and push the least whit more. His heart was like a great puffed ball, pushing with unimaginable agony against his ribs, that pushed it back and cut into it like knives, inflicting yet more agonies.

Yet all that lasted through the space of only seven breaths.

Then the Cauldron burst, and the heart of Evnissyen burst with it.

The men of the Island of the Mighty, in that hill-high House of Bran, heard a crash as of the moon breaking and falling in fragments upon the earth. They rushed out in time to see a great mass of fire rising from the hill of their foes; then it flew apart and fell back, like a rain of flames, upon Tara.

The Cauldron of the Gods had gone back to the land of the Gods.

Bran said, "He did one good deed at the last. I am glad of that; for his sake as well as ours, for he was our young brother, and fair to look upon. He gave his life for the lives of all of us, and no man can do more than that."

"He did according to his nature to the last," said Manawyddan. "He saved us by destruction, that is his one gift."

All night long the druids labored upon the scorched, seared ramparts of Tara, every art they knew exerted to turn aside the fumes that had been freed by the bursting of the Cauldron. Like a tawny cloud these hovered over the land of Ireland; thick rolling mists shot with a strange fiery green, with purple, and with orange; and whatever color glowed flamelike or wriggled snakelike through those grisly vapors was, when seen there, hideous, a horror to the eyes of men.

Death was in them, those fumes of the Underworld. Birds fell from heaven, cattle died in the fields and foxes in their dens. So did the people, the nobles in their fine wooden houses and the poor folk in their clumsy huts of stone. By dawn no life was left in all that wide plain that stretches westward from Tara of the Kings; no man or woman or beast survived, save in Tara's ancient holy self, and in the House of Bran.

Such was the fruit of the sacrifice of Evnissyen, that strangest of the saviors of men.

He had come and gone, that dark diseased soul whom the druids had foretold. He had shattered a world as he had shattered the Cauldron whose shape symbolized the world, and his own darkness, dissolving into the elements more quickly than his broken body, may have helped to poison those fumes. Though with what unknowable powers his essence blended none can ever guess, what forces lurked in that Cauldron alien to earth: the giver of Life that, carried away by sacrilege, had passed through the Pass of the Dog's Mouth and become a poisoned, perverted shadow of itself.

He was gone, and with him had passed the world he had known. But his brothers did not yet know that, they who labored through the night as the Irish druids labored. They did know what gift he had died to give them, they to whose druid sight his last thoughts must have been visible, agonized images fading into the mists that had engulfed him.

All through the night the sons of Llyr labored, and in the morning they saw that they had saved all of their men who still could stand; but the more sorely wounded had died where they lay. Ever since her son's death, Branwen had lived for the need of those hurt men; it had given her refuge from her own pain, strength to hold shut the doors of past and future. Now she sat desolate, her red, ruined hands empty in her lap, her eyes emptier. In that gray dawn her brothers saw fully, for the first time, what those years in the pit had done to her.

Bran turned away his face, and in his eyes was sorrow beyond all telling. Then he looked at the brother and at the men who were left to him.

"Let us send a herald to Matholuch," he said. "Tell him that we take our sister and leave this land. His people cannot wish for more battle now, any more than ours do."

And in the worn faces all around him hope dawned, feeble maybe as the light that shone upon the corpse-strewn land outside, but still hope. *Home,* they thought.

Home. Before their eyes rose visions of green fields they knew, of the faces of friends and kin. *It will be the same.*

They thought they could do what no man or woman has yet done, and go back into the past.

The herald went, and the others, tired as they were, almost feverishly set about gathering together and packing their possessions. Only Branwen still sat like a carved figure, with her quiet, empty hands.

Manawyddan went to her at last and said, "Will you pack for us, sister? Bran and I have much else to do." She rose at once, smiled at him with her mouth and set to work, but though her hands were busy her eyes were still empty.

But Bran's eyes grew easier as he watched her. He said to Manawyddan, "It will heal her, our own land. The smell of the white hawthorne and the purple heather, and the sight of the sunlight on the cliffs of Harlech. She is too young not to go on. Not to want a man again, and feel how like a harp the body is when love moves it to music. Not to bear more children. However her heart is scarred, can any dead child's scream in the fire ring as loud in a mother's ears as the living child's cry for her teat? Home and time are all Branwen needs; life itself will do the rest."

"I hope so," said Manawyddan. He thought, *But home itself will be different, brother. Grief will come on many faces when they look at the few who still follow us and see that their own men are not there. Not until we are old can we hope to see again such a glorious crowd of young men as shouted once beneath the heights of Harlech.*

For many years now much of the Island of the Mighty would be a land of women. Those who had been girls with Branwen would be weeping for their brothers, and for the fathers of their children. She would know herself for the cause of that weeping; certainly that would not help to heal her wounds.

If they could still be healed . . .

The herald came back from Tara. The Irish had not been friendly, but they had been glad to know that soon the strangers would be gone from their island.

One more night what had been the host of Bran slept in the House of Bran. In the morning they would set out.

The moon shone down; coldly, upon a ruined land. In the hall of Tara what nobles the men of Ireland had left came to Matholuch.

"Lord," they said, "you are King over a land of the dead. Maybe in the far north, in Ulster the stronghold of the Old Tribes, some folk are left alive. Maybe on the western shores, where the storms beat forever, there are yet others. We do not know; but there cannot be many anywhere. Neither do we know whether our poisoned fields will bear grass or crops again, or whether the few women we have left can still bear us babes. Children we have none—all were blasted."

"That is so," said Matholuch. He thought, *You have not come here only to tell me that which I already knew.* And stiffened with an old dread.

They looked at him with savage eyes, those few who were left him, those always savage captains of the New Tribes. The hard eyes of men who think they have nothing left to lose.

"Shall we let them go, Lord? To laugh at us?"

Matholuch said heavily, "It will be long before they laugh. Of those who crossed the sea not more than one out of ten can still be living. We have made them pay dear for their coming."

"Yet in the Island of the Mighty they may grow great again, may come back with a fresh host—many men must have been left behind to see to their farms and towns—to take this land that they have made a waste. Make it theirs forever."

Matholuch licked his lips. He said wearily, "What would you have me do?" This was an old story . . .

"Let us follow them, Lord. Ambush them on their way to their ships. Two of the royal brothers are already dead. If we could get the heads of the other two—! Or even your woman's own, she that sat and watched her son burn . . ."

Matholuch remembered Branwen's face as it had looked when she saw that burning; heard the screams again, hers and the boy's. For a breath's space something seemed to swing back and forth inside him; almost it got free.

He said harshly, "Speak no more of that. He that burned was my son." Almost he had said, "Speak no more of her," and if he had got that one word out maybe he would have been a man, he who had given up his manhood that he might stay a king.

He remained a king; the king he had always been. He said, "But we will follow them. Yes, we will follow them."

In the morning the men of Bran set forth. It was a chilly, misty morning. Gray heavy rain clouds had followed those poisonous fiery vapors, as though earth tried to heal herself; but as yet no rain had fallen.

Bran looked back once at his house and laughed. "I will never go inside a house again," he said. Had Branwen not been within hearing he would have added, "Would that I never had seen this one." He did say, "All I will ever ask for again is the sky that arches over the Island of the Mighty. That is cover enough for my head."

All were tired and hurt, but all applauded. *Home!*

He marched off, his men around him.

Halfway to the sea it happened. There was a wood, and its leaves were withered; what greenness the coming winter had left, the Cauldron's fumes had charred and blackened. From beneath those ruined trees came death: a shower of spears like low-flying, bronze-beaked birds, and after them, with earsplitting howls, the Irish.

In that last battle the men of the Island of the Mighty fought as a great stag fights, surrounded by dogs, and the others fought like what they were—men whose wives and children, kin and homes and goods, all had perished by that smoky death. Men whose world had ended and who were willing to end with it if they could end the destroyers, the bringers of the doom.

Bran drove the Irish back into the wood. Like the giant he was he pushed forward, his sword whirling like grim light around him, until the black tree shadows engulfed him, reaching for him like the long black arms of giants mightier even than he. A great spear came from behind and pierced his thigh, but he fought on, the haft protruding from his flesh. Twenty more men fell by him before the poison on its point reached his great heart and he fell.

Over the body of their King his men made their last stand. All but seven of them died there, the *Mabinogi* says; and the names of those seven will never be forgotten so long as the Island of the Mighty remembers the glory of her youth: Manawyddan the King's brother, Ynawc, Grudyen, Gluneu, Taliesin, later to be famed for his many births, Pryderi Prince of Dyved, and Heilyn son of Gwynn the Ancient.

The Irish died to the last man.

They were faint and heartsick, those seven who were left. Through the gray rain that had at last begun to fall they stumbled and struggled, striving to build a fire and keep it alight, striving to build some kind of shelter, with broken branches and dead men's cloaks, above Bran where he lay. Branwen helped them, she whom Manawyddan and Pryderi had covered with their shields to the last.

Bran was alive, though he could not move. Like a net of fire the poison filled his veins, and like ice it froze bone and muscle. He suffered much, and all knew that there was no hope.

Stone-still and stone-white, Branwen tended him. Only her eyes were still alive, and all the life in them was misery.

"Sorrow on the day that I sent the starling, brother," she said, and her voice was flat and dull as the blade of a tarnished knife. "I never thought to remember those days in the pit as happy, but how glad I would be to toil in its heat now and think that my baby lived, and that you lived."

He could not touch her. He looked at her with eyes that were as tender as any touch.

"Do not blame yourself, Branwen, girl. On me alone the blame is. I never should have sent you into Ireland; I failed in wisdom, and what is worse, I failed in love— both to you and to our people—and may my blood alone, and not my son's blood, be required in payment! But I do not know—I do not know . . .

"You do not understand, you cannot. Be it so. Only do not weep, small Branwen, for your tears are the one thing that are as bitter as the poison. Both together are more than I can bear."

She winked the tears off her lashes. She set her teeth and schooled herself again to stone.

"Evil indeed would it be of me not to do that much for you, Bran, brother—I that have cost you your life."

"You have not," said Bran. He looked at Manawyddan, grinned a little, with his pain-wrung mouth.

"Tell her, brother, you who know it all and fought it all. But do not tell her until I am dead, for it is uncomfortable enough I am already, without seeing her eyes when she knows."

He said later, "I tore my own pattern—I pulled down, whose work it was to build . . ."

Then his eyes closed and for awhile he seemed to dream, and they sat around him quiet as the falling shadows, thanking the Gods and the Mothers that so, however briefly, he could rest.

Manawyddan kept his arm around Branwen, and her body yielded to the comfort of that hold, but her face still stared unseeingly into misery, with eyes that would never see the good common outer world again.

The night wore. Dawn came, gray and sorrowful. Then suddenly the far east glowed golden, like a door opening into the Shining World.

Bran opened his eyes. He looked, with patient, harried eyes, toward that gold. He said, "I should like to see the sun again; take me outside. It is bad luck houses have always been to me, from the day that I could not get into them until I got into this one—no blame to you, sister, for having it built."

They saw that he thought that he was still inside that house the Irish had built. They lifted him and carried him into the open, clear of the shadow of the trees.

He looked around him happily. "Thank you, men. I will die out here where I can feel the life of earth around me, where everything is always dying, changing, taking new shapes to live again. Walls stay dead forever. What man makes and not the Mothers, that alone can change only to decay; Their handiwork is ever-living."

Then the pain came back and he writhed.

"It is not to be easy then . . . Branwen? Where is the girl?"

Branwen had stayed behind in the dark. Bran looked back and saw her in that miserable shelter that now seemed like a door into darkness, and the saddest of all his looks was on his face.

"Girl, come here. No—" as Manawyddan, gray-lipped now with understanding, would have stopped him. "No. Why should I escape and leave you that burden too? The telling as well as the doing."

She came and he spoke to her. "Branwen, it is brave you must be. I am in too much pain to bear it any longer, and if I could there may still be some Irish left somewhere, and you that can live should be getting back to the ships."

She could not go whiter. She said nothing, only looked at him with dark eyes as piteous as though he had been about to pronounce her own doom.

He smiled into them. "You would not wish to keep me suffering when I could be well, Branwen?"

She bowed her head. He looked into the whitening faces of the men around him and they shrank back.

"Cut off my head," he said. "Whichever of you loves me best, though I think that one of you should be willing to spare my brother, who does."

They shrank farther back.

"Lord," said Ynawc, moistening his trembling lips, "we are not traitors. How could we do this thing to you?"

"You are my men," said Bran. "You cannot be traitors so long as you do my bidding."

"Then we are very loving traitors, Lord," said Pryderi. "We cannot do your bidding. I do not see how it could be done. Be a good lord to us," he urged, with his winning smile, "as you always have been, and do not ask it of us."

Bran ignored that smile, though it had got round most people all Pryderi's life long.

"I have asked it," said Bran. "Is it love to leave me in this pain?"

Manawyddan set his jaw and came forward. "I will do it," he said.

"That is what I expected," Bran said. "Good, wise Manawyddan; always dreading and foreseeing the hard thing that would not happen if you were listened to and always setting your shoulder to it when it has come. That is some men's luck in life."

Pryderi flushed scarlet and his hands clenched. He stepped forward. "Is there none of you that will spare his brother the deed, when that is the last thing the King asked of us?" He looked hopefully round the circle, but met only silence. "If there is not," he said and squared his shoulders, and his mouth tightened and grew white, "I will do it myself."

But Manawyddan had always a tenderness for that gay young king of Dyved. He smiled at him now.

"Your youth is the one brightness left on our earth, Pryderi; I would not have a cloud put on it before one must come. Take Branwen away, lad; that you can do. Go all of you, and leave us sons of Llyr alone."

They went, Branwen walking rigidly; the marks her nails made in her palms then were to be there till her death day. All her thought was, *I must not make it harder for either of them.* She was a will, no longer a woman.

When Manawyddan raised the sword, Bran smiled up into his eyes. "Long ago, Manawyddan, you told me that I who was so fond of building new roads might build a road that would break my neck. It breaks now. Who knows? When we get another birth I may heed you more, my best friend and my brother, son of Llyr."

Five men went on, with Branwen and the head, toward the ships. Manawyddan and Pryderi stayed behind to heap the cairn high over the body that had been Bran the Blessed's. It was wet, dreary work; the gray rain had begun again.

When it was done, Manawyddan looked toward the wood. "There is one more task to be done, boy."

Pryderi found his smile that for hours had been lost. His white teeth flashed in it, pearl-bright.

"Indeed I have been thinking of that, Lord," he said. "And hoping that you would let me have a hand in it."

They went together into the wood. They threaded their way among dead men, and among blasted trees and bushes. Until Pryderi gave a cry and stopped.

"I thought the spear must have been thrown from about here." There was no need to say which spear. "And it was! See . . ."

He held out a bit of red cloth that had been caught upon a branch; red cloth from a man's cloak; a cloak they knew.

"Branwen wove this and embroidered it." Manawyddan's face did not change as he took the rag. "Strange that he still wore it."

"You knew that it was he—?" Pryderi stared.

"He was not among the dead. Also last night I felt him fleeing; felt his triumph and his fear."

For a breath's space Pryderi was silent, awed. The New Tribes saw only with the eyes in their faces; they had not that other sight that the Old Tribes had— that sight that came and went, and often was not there, but could be such a thing of dread.

Then he laughed shortly. "Well, it is still true that the Irish died to the last man. He is good at dodging men, that King who is not quite a man. Will he find a way not quite to die?"

"Not with us behind him." Manawyddan's voice was as unchanging as his face.

They went on through the wood; they came out on the other side of it. The rain stopped and the moon shone. Pale as a ghost of the sun it shone down upon a desolate land, a land that lay as devoid of life as all lands may have lain before life was created. The birds lay dead beneath the trees, and the beasts in the fields. A woman lay dead beside a well, a fallen bucket beside her; also a fallen child. Not even an ant was there to feed on their discarded flesh.

But somewhere in all that stillness still lurked one living thing . . .

The rain had washed away all tracks, yet somehow Manawyddan knew which way to go. Perhaps the feverish heat of his quarry's own fear guided him, as the hare's smell guides the hounds. In the dawn at last they found him, asleep under some bushes. These might have hidden him, had he not still been wrapped in his torn red cloak, that made him look as though mantled in blood.

They stood and looked down upon him, and knew that the chase was over.

Manawyddan's face was set, as it had been set ever since that moment in which he drew his sword and advanced upon Bran. Set as a face carved in stone. He drew his sword again, but there was no joy in his eyes.

"The druids would say that I still had much to learn," he said. "They would be right. This will not bring Bran back. But it must be done. This that lies here has done more and brought about more than I can bear."

"Lord," said Pryderi very hopefully, "I remember that you never liked killing, and it is glad indeed I would be to step on this louse for you. So if you do not want to bother . . ."

"There is still a king to be killed," said Manawyddan, "and I will do it who for this hour and never again am a king, Beli's heir."

He put the point of his sword against Matholuch's throat and stirred him, not roughly, with his foot.

Matholuch started wide-awake. As though even in his sleep he had expected this, feared it and waited. His terrified eyes darted from side to side, from one man to the other, like trapped beasts.

"Manawyddan!" he said. "Brother! It was not I that killed Bran. It was not by my order that the man hid and did it. It never has been by my will that harm has been done to any of you, to my lady or to her brothers, my kin. Manawyddan, remember that we are one kin . . ."

"Rise up," said Manawyddan, "you who struck the weak in the face and the strong in the back."

But Matholuch the Mouse-Hearted had no mind to get up, even when the sword pricked a little deeper. Pryderi began to draw his.

"Indeed, Lord, now that we have caught our mouse, is there any need for us to play cats with him, because he will not act like a man? Let us kill him at once, like men."

Matholuch shrieked at that, he flung up begging, clawing hands. He had none of the props of pride left, and therefore no pride; he had no vanity; he had only flesh that wanted to go on breathing.

"Manawyddan, Manawyddan—" The words were a prayer.

Then he met those gray eyes that were as deep as the sea and as cold, and his tongue froze in his mouth. For a long moment there was silence, there in the dawn; the sun was rising bloodily in the east.

"O man of almosts," said Manawyddan, "this is the end of you. Rise up now and do one deed wholly; you have never done that, for even when you were born there did not quite enough of you come to make a man. Die like one now, give my sister, who has lain with you, one decency to remember; do not put more shame than you must on the memory of my nephew, whom you fathered. Die decently, for there is no way out of dying; I will not let you live."

Matholuch rose up then. He swallowed hard, three times; his tongue came alive and he licked his lips with it, though it was only a poor frightened thing, shivering there in the dry red cave of his mouth.

Pryderi stood watchful, his sword ready in case of tricks. But there were no more tricks in Matholuch; he had no cunning left. An end of all things had come to him, and here was the end of himself.

He fought, and he did not do badly in that last battle. The sun was high in the east when Manawyddan killed him. It beat upon his face as he fell, and turned his almost red hair and beard to gold. It gleamed in his glazed eyes, that looked straight up, at last without fear.

Manawyddan wiped his sword, and sheathed it.

"Are you not going to take his head, Lord?" Pryderi looked in surprise from those dead eyes to Manawyddan's, that were unreadable, gray and cold.

"No," said Manawyddan. "Branwen shall not look upon his face again. Besides, we have heads enough to carry. One head—I would not pair that with this."

13

The Wind of Death

Through that night the five men from the Island of the Mighty had slept, exhausted, upon the cold seashore.

They had come to that shore, and they had found all changed. Their ships were wrecked or gone. The Sinking Lands no longer stretched like a marshy bridge from Ireland to the Island of the Mighty. They had sunk in that mighty catastrophe when the Cauldron had burst and its venomed fumes had spread over earth and sea.

Dead among the wreckage of the ships lay those few men who had been left to guard them. While war raged the outnumbered Irish had spared them; the older and cooler heads among them cannot have wished to cut off the enemy's retreat. But that cloud of death had spared nothing.

Weary and wounded as they were, the five men built a funeral pyre for the comrades they had hoped would welcome them. Then they made camp, as best they could. With the hulls of two broken boats they made a shelter for Branwen, and in it with her they set the Head of Bran, in the golden dish in which they had carried it, that dish which had been brought from Harlech to hold his food.

They slept then, but Branwen did not sleep. She knew what errand must be keeping the one brother she had left, and in the dark she lay and prayed to the Mothers.

"Let him be safe—let nothing happen to Manawyddan, my brother . . . Let the man who once was my man die better than he has lived . . ."

Would Manawyddan bring that head back upon a pole, dead eyes glazed above the gray lips that once had been warm on hers? And if he did, what would she do? Smite that cold cheek as once he had smitten hers, the outland coward, her brother's slayer? Or go mad and take it down off the spike and cradle it where it had wished to lie—for its own safety's sake, not for any love of her—that head of the father of her son? No, never that; he had killed Bran.

Bran! Bran, my brother! Gwern, my baby! You two I loved, and him I learned to hate, yet now that I too am guilty and broken I can see the terribleness of having to hate him of all men—Matholuch! I would have pitied Gwern if he had been afraid, yet his father I could not pity. A man should be a man. Not a walking, twisting fear.

Oh, Bran, my brother! Gwern, my son!

She prayed again. *"Mothers, keep Manawyddan safe."* But she could not feel the Mothers. She could feel only the great dark about her, the darkness that seemed as vast as the world. Both Those she prayed to and those she prayed for seemed as far away as the stars, and she was all alone, shipwrecked and solitary forever.

Then out of the darkness the Head of Bran spoke. "You are not alone, small Branwen. I am here."

She raised herself on one arm. She stared, no more breath in her than in the Head.

Its eyes had opened, and they were Bran's eyes. Its lips opened, it spoke again, and the voice was the old deep voice that had been Bran's when it was upon his shoulders.

"Child, not yet can I go to my rest, who have brought all of you to this."

She cried out at that. "No! I brought *you* here. To your death."

But the Head only smiled. "Girl, Matholuch and his butcher left you one ear; use it. He took you to get a son who would be King of the Island of the Mighty, and I cheated him, who hoped that if your boy was born afar Caradoc might be King after me. You were the pawn in the game we played. You have little to thank us for, husband or brother."

For a breath's space her eyes widened, but then memory overwhelmed her again.

"I had Gwern. Another man might have given me another son, but not him, and I cannot wish him unborn. Weakling though his father was, only we two together could have made *him*."

"You two made his body, girl; not all of him."

"The body that Evnissyen burned!" That memory tore a scream from her; she rocked back and forth, moaning. "Go to your rest, Bran; take me with you! Then I may find him again. He may be remembering— he was so little, he cannot understand what happened that night. Even in the arms of the Mothers he cannot understand. What if he thinks, like the Irish, that all of us betrayed him, even I . . ."

"Peace, sister! He needs no comfort. That burning

was only an evil dream. Evnissyen made all of us dream it, but Gwern was the first to wake."

"But he is gone. I cannot see him, I cannot hold him. I can see only his death—hear only his cry; day and night, sleeping and waking, I am burning with that sight and with that sound! I am dying, yet I cannot die. Give me rest, Bran; let us both rest!" She still rocked to and fro.

"Girl, these are only evil dreams; you torture yourself for nothing. In the pit you had courage to work and wait and be patient. Have that courage again."

"To what end, Brother? Oh, I know—I do not doubt what the druids say. Sometime I shall find my son again—but when, and what forms will we wear? I want my baby—not a strange man, or some shining spirit—and him I will never have again. Three years I waited—three hard bitter years, praying the Mothers not to let him change too much—and now I must wait again! For a stranger."

"You want the image that you cherished in the pit, Branwen; his chubbiness and roundness, the curls that you combed, and the arms that he put round your neck. But those things you may have again in another child; they are things that always pass. Not the true Gwern."

"I want the Gwern I knew!"

She wept until at last the Head wept with her; then she roused herself, and pitied its sorrow as she would have pitied the living Bran's. She wiped its eyes, where the tears trickled down the great face to the chin, and she tried to wipe away the blood that ringed its neck, but she could not, for that blood always stayed fresh. As she worked the Head watched her, and that look was not quite like the living Bran's.

"Sleep, Branwen," it said gently. "It is true that you need rest, little sister. Lie down and sleep."

Hope kindled in her white face. "You mean . . ."

"No. Your body is still too strong for that. But sleep, and if your sorrow does not bind your mind too fast to your body, you will find Gwern again, even though when you wake you may not remember the meeting."

"I must wake?" Her mouth trembled, her eyes were sick with pain.

But the Head looked at her, and under that strange compelling gaze, weights seemed to come upon her eyelids; she fell down where his feet should have been and slept. And the Head still looked down upon her, and its eyes were sad for her, and for all things.

"Evnissyen, can you bear to look on this, from where you are, you that burned her child's body in the fire and burn her spirit in it yet? Oh, the deed is hers also, that yields herself to the fires you kindled, but she is not the first of our blood to love a son too much. All these deeds sprang from my deed, and for me the time of payment draws near . . .

"Some day folk will believe in a God Who burns men forever and ever, and they will call Him a God of Love—and then as now, themselves will still burn themselves. When will there be an end of burning, O Mothers? An end of the pain we children of women deal each other?"

And the Head looked toward the east, where the Island of the Mighty was. Out across the foam-tipped, troubled billows of the dark sea it looked, and through the moonlit darkness above. How far those strange eyes saw no man may tell, but agony rose through their calm, and for a space they were but the eyes of Bran looking upon his own misery.

"*Caradoc,*" the Head said softly. "*Caradoc.*"

In the Town of the Seven Chiefs, Caradoc sat with

the Six. They were happy, because the storms and the undersea crashings that had come with the final subsidence of the Sinking Lands were over. Land and sea were at peace again.

The *Mabinogi* says that Pendaran Dyved was there, as a young page. But that seems strange, for Pendaran Dyved must have been an old man then. He cannot have been young twenty years before, when, as Pwyll's chief druid, he named Pryderi from that first cry Rhiannon gave when she knew that her longed-for little son was safe. "Now I am relieved of my anxiety (*pryde ri*)." Most likely his druid sight had warned him of danger (between Dyved's princes and the Children of Llyr the bonds were always close), and he had left his own body behind in Dyved and come to borrow the page's for awhile. The lad's own spirit must have gone where sleeping folk go.

The Seven feasted, and the druid watched, wise eyes of age shining with the brightness of those borrowed young ones, and the night wore. The moon came down from her throne, and the heavens darkened; the earth shivered as if before the coming of vast cold. Inside Caradoc's hall was still light and warmth, but outside, in that last starless hush before the dawn, blackness lay like a great beast crouching at the doors.

"Lord, the wind is rising." The youth who had Pendaran Dyved inside him spoke to Caradoc. "Shall I shut the doors?"

Caradoc laughed and shook his head. "I feel no draught, boy. I never have known a stiller night."

"It is too still, Lord. The wind will be a great one when it comes."

Unic Glew laughed drunkenly. "Run along, youngster—have a drink and warm yourself. We have had enough winds lately; we do not want you scaring up more out of your head."

The page made no answer. He stood and eyed those doors that were all darknesses: watching eyes of night.

Heveydd the Tall and Gwlch drowsed; they were the oldest of the seven chiefs. But Iddic, sitting near them, stirred restlessly of a sudden. He ran his hand over the back of his neck.

"Hoo! That was a wind! Cold as a knife. Maybe those doors need shutting, after all."

Fodor the son of Ervyll was sitting next to Iddic. He started, looked behind him, then shook his yellow hair out of his eyes and laughed.

"You are right, Iddic. That was a wind! There must be many dead riding on it, to make it so cold. I hope our ships are safe, there in Ireland. It is a good thing that your father's new palace is too far inland, Caradoc, to have been flooded."

Llassar the son of Llassar frowned. He was the greatest warrior there, and he sat next to Caradoc.

"We may have missed a messenger from Ireland. Not one from your father, Caradoc—this fellow asked for me. But he must have known something about the host."

"Who? When? How?" There was an instant pricking of ears, a raising of heads. Caradoc's eager voice cut across them all. "Who was the man, Llassar? And how did you miss his message?"

"Because he died, Lord. Died saying, 'Llassar. Tell Llassar—' But what he would have told me only Arawn, King of the Underworld, knows."

"How did it happen?"

"My men found him on the seashore, beside the wreckage of a fishing boat."

"You think he had been caught in the sinking—?" Caradoc drew a deep breath. Awesome indeed was the thought of that convulsed sea, of the depths opening and swallowing up their long-awaited prey.

Llassar said simply, "No man could have lived through that, Lord."

"You have no idea who he was?"

"He could have been anybody but a small man, Lord, or one as big as your father. He had been a warrior, no fisherman; he had worn gold and scarlet, and he was covered with wounds, old and new. He was built like my brothers, Kueli and half-faced Keli, but whether he was one or either of them not even my mother, Kymideu Kymeinvoll, could have told. He had no face left at all."

"You think the sea had done that?"

Llassar said slowly, "No. Men must have fallen upon him just after he landed. Maybe he mistook them for friends. It was still dark when my men found him, yesterday morning, and they swear that they heard fleeing footsteps."

Caradoc frowned. "Robbers? I thought we had cleaned all of them out of these parts. But his news cannot have been important; no messenger from the King my father would have come alone and in a fishing boat."

Yet he still frowned, uneasy. No man could have wished to make that voyage. Even when no terrors rose out of the deep, that wild, already wintry sea was cruel to travelers. Bran and his men, with their fleet, would be mad, to try to come home before spring warmed the winds and the waters. Yet one man alone had dared that journey—and when the sea could not yet fully have subsided after making its terrible and titanic meal. What fear, what need, could have driven him?

Can harm have come to the host? To my father—? Firmly Caradoc told himself that that thought was folly.

He shrugged. "Well, it is a strange business. But we

must catch those robbers; I will not have more men killed."

Iddic looked up from his wine again. His eyes had a strange glitter, a glaze, like the beginning of emptiness. "It must have been he that I felt riding upon the wind. Your brother, Llassar. Why should he run his cold hand along the back of my neck? Keli never liked me— why should he come to me first? But your turn will come."

Llassar said sharply, "There is no proof that that dead man was Keli my brother."

Caradoc said, "We will send for a druid. One powerful enough to call him back and find out who he was. We will send into Dyved for Pendaran Dyved himself, if need be."

"I wish he could hold the fellow long enough to find out what his message was," Fodor muttered.

A mighty wind suddenly blew through the hall. The candle flames twisted, sank, and for a breath's space the long room seemed to tip over into darkness. Even the fire upon the hearth shrank down, as if in fear of hands that might seize it. Then the flames rose again; all was as before.

Caradoc said abruptly to the disguised druid, "That was a better idea of yours than we thought, boy. I would not have that draught come again. Shut the doors."

The druid did not move. He was staring hard into the shadows, as though trying to find in that dark, clustering troop one that might have life in it, a thicker, stronger shade.

"Too late, Lord," he whispered. "Too late. It is inside now. We do not want to shut ourselves in with It."

"With what?" Unic Glew laughed loudly. "You heard the King's son, boy. Go and get those doors shut." And he made a pass at the seeming boy's head.

The druid did not even bother to dodge, as any real boy would have done. He still stared into the shadows. "Listen."

Outside a great storm broke suddenly. The black waiting stillness turned into raging sound. Wind shrieked round the house. Hail battered it, beating upon the roof like a myriad tiny, frantic hands.

Fodor whispered, "So it storms when the mighty die. When a man's Other World foes and friends fight around his house."

Caradoc went white to the lips. "If this means that harm has come to my father—or to my uncles . . ."

Iddic had still been staring with dulled eyes into his wine. Now suddenly he raised his head.

"So it is you, Keli? I thought so. No—you are trying to warn me? It is . . ."

As he spoke there was a flash of light and his head fell, and blood rose in a spurting jet from his neck.

His head fell upon the table before him and rolled along it, the eyes glazing now into complete emptiness.

For a space all men saw the sword that had flashed through the air to smite him; then, lightning-like as it had come, it flashed back into nothingness.

They had seen no hand. . . .

Fodor mab Ervyll screamed. He sprang up, away from the headless sitting body of Iddic. But even as he did so, even as that body crumpled, the sword flashed once more. It went through his back and out again through his breast; and mighty must have been the tug that drew it out again.

It dripped in the air and vanished, as if dissolving.

Fodor fell and lay still; and the relaxing body of Iddic fell and sprawled across him, limply as a dropped doll falls from a child's hand.

Llassar sprang forward, across them both, and struck madly with his own sword into the air from which that shining death had come. But his blade found nothing.

So for a little while he dueled with air; and the others ran hither and thither, striking about them with their swords. But they saw nothing, heard nothing; they smote only air, pierced only air.

Caradoc moved toward Llassar. "Back to back! If we stand so we cannot be reached from all sides at once. Back to back, men!"

He shouted, but they did not hear him. They leaped and ducked and sidestepped, they fled from corners and they dived into corners, crouching there and swinging their swords in fierce circles before them, to keep off that unseen foe.

Caradoc reached Llassar. And in that very moment the sword came out of the air again. Behind Llassar the son of Llassar, not before him. Blood from the blade spattered Caradoc's cheek as it clove downward, through Llassar's shoulder, to his heart.

He fell, and his weight bore Caradoc to the ground with him. The druid flinched, expecting to see the blade pierce that prostrate body, but once more it vanished. Caradoc stumbled to his feet, untouched.

"To the doors, men! Let us get out!"

They heard him this time, in the brief, dreadful silence that followed Llassar's fall. They rushed for the doors and he rushed with them, but between them and that sheltering darkness the sword flashed again, dripping now with the blood of three men.

Caradoc sprang at it; his own blade struck against it. "Smite, men! It cannot hold the door against all of us. There is a body somewhere behind it . . ."

But as he spoke the sword vanished, and then came again; and there came a terrible groaning scream from Gwlch. He crumpled to his knees; the sword flashed and dripped as it left his breast.

All courage seemed to leave them then, those last

two chieftains, those warriors who had been brave in battle, Unic Glew and Heveydd, called the Tall. Like mice played with by an invisible cat they fled through the hall, their swords whirling round them. Caradoc followed them, but they paid him no heed; more than once their swords almost spitted him.

Backed against the wall, the page who was Pendaran Dyved stood silently watching, his old eyes showing through his young face, like a reflection under water . . .

That came which must come. The sword appeared in the air again, this time above Caradoc's head. Even as the druid shouted warning, even as his last two men jumped back, screaming, it crashed down through flesh and bone.

It pierced the thigh of Heveydd the Tall, and as he stumbled, dropping down awkwardly to the height of other men, it flashed again, smote again. The once high head of Heveydd bounced from his shoulders, and past the cheek of Caradoc.

Of the six chieftains five had fallen.

Only Unic Glew was left, and unfortunately his courage came back to him. He lurched about uncertainly in his drunkenness, trying to balance himself on legs that did not seem very well acquainted. Again and again he stabbed the air.

"Unic! Unic Glew!" Caradoc called him, but he only shook his head dizzily and went on stabbing shadows.

"Let me alone, son of Bran. The sword lets you alone—time after time that has been shown. You need no help and you can give no help. Let us fighters be."

He stabbed another shadow. "I have never run from a man with a sword," he mumbled with dignity, "and I am through running from a sword with no man onto it."

He walked out into the middle of the hall.

Caradoc knew what would happen then. What five

times already that night he had seen happen, and he could not bear it. Within him something snapped, as an overtaut cord snaps. He sprang after Unic Glew and hurled him against the wall, covering him with his own body. With straining eyes he stared into and begged that deadly Nothingness:

"If you will not fight me like a man, at least let me die with my men. Do not put this shame on me, to see all of them die before my eyes while I strike no blow."

But nothing answered him. No sound, no movement, no flash of sword. The candles burned lower. The hail still beat upon the roof, frantic as helpers, defenders, that could not get in.

From his place against the wall the druid watched as quietly as God . . .

Caradoc threw back his head, so that his throat and breast made a target, defenseless and bared.

"Are you a coward to ignore a challenge? It is in my keeping this island was left; it is under me those six were. Take my life, and let this last man go."

He saw the sword coming. Like a ray of light it advanced, here glittering bronze, there the fresh scarlet of dripping blood.

He stood steady to meet it, eyes alert, sword ready. And then Unic struggled and twisted away from the wall.

"Here it comes! Let me at it, boy."

Caradoc tried to push him back, and in the struggle Unic's back was turned, and the sword flashed down into it. In horror Caradoc's hands fell, and Unic broke free and staggered back to one of the long tables. He clutched it, staring with astounded eyes at Caradoc.

"You held me—for it to stab me."

Those were his last words. He fell then and died.

The stiffening corpse lay there, and Caradoc lay

beside it. The rain blew in gusts through the hall, and beat upon the breast that he had bared to the sword in vain.

Sometimes he talked to himself, and his voice and the shrieking wind were the only sounds that broke that silence.

"It is in my keeping that my father left the Island of the Mighty, and this is how I have kept it. What man would follow me now? I am all alone . . .

"Six times my heart has been pierced this night, and yet I live. All of them, all of them!" He named their names, and ground his teeth, and wept. "Yes, *I* live— my life he counts too poor a thing to take! And he has made it so . . . If I could get at him, if I could see him, for but one breath's space! There is no distance I could not spring across to seize him, no sword and no strength that could help him, once my hands were on him! But I cannot see him, I cannot reach him! He will only kill and kill, and let me live and watch . . . May the Hounds of Arawn tear him, may his soul hang red and ragged from their jaws!

"I can do nothing, I cannot find him, I cannot ask more men to follow me to a death that I cannot share. It is poor stuff for a king I am. Caradoc the cursed, son of Bran the Blessed."

The silent walls seemed to echo that in many voices, the rain that had followed the hail seemed to beat it out with tiny feet upon the hard-trod floor, thousands of sounds forged in the flaming anvil of his tortured brain into one sound:

"Caradoc the Cursed . . . Caradoc the Cursed!"

He lay there and his mind burned and his body burned.

He lay there and he died there, before dawn.

Morning came, and out of its gray shadows the

earth reshaped herself, black formlessness and mis-shapenness taking on form and warmth and color. Out of those gray shadows where the dead men lay and the druid crouched, the form of the magician took on shape and humanity and color. He stood there a living man, clean and comely, save for his bloodstained sword.

He was Caswallon, the son of Beli.

He walked over to the dead son of Bran. He knelt and felt over him with his hands, then looked up at the still silent druid.

"This is not my doing; my hands are free of kindred blood. It would have hurt my heart to slay him, because he was my nephew, my cousin's son, and indeed there is no mark on him. You will bear witness to that, druid."

"You did not shed his blood. To that I will bear witness."

"I did not plan this; I did not foresee it. How could I have foreseen it? I never would have died only because other men died; it seems to me that the boy was a great fool."

"He will be called one of the Three Chief Guardians who died of vexation and grief. The *Triads* will give him that name and honor him long after both of us are dust."

"Who will the other two Guardians be?" A shadow crossed Caswallon's face.

"They will not be of your blood. No son of yours will reign after you. The Island of the Mighty will have many kings now, but none will reign in peace, and none will found a dynasty. And in the end fair-haired invaders will sweep over all and subject us all— New Tribes and Old alike. Bran might have prevented that had he not given away his sister and the Cauldron, that symbol of the cup within her body—the power of birth and rebirth, the power of woman. Now for ages women will be as beasts of the field and we men will rule, and practice war, our art. By it we will live—or by it, rather, we will struggle and die."

"For awhile at least I will rule, druid. Who are you? Math the Ancient?"

"I am Pendaran Dyved. Math's spells would have been strong enough to tear the Veil of Illusion from you. It was your good fortune—or your bad—that he never crosses the borders of Gwynedd, his trust from the Mothers."

"It was my good fortune—if he would have been strong enough. I am not bloodthirsty; I will be a good friend to all who pay me due homage as High King. I will not even harm those who do not, so long as they do not lift hand against me. I think they will be few."

"Did Keli lift his hand against you? He that came to warn his brothers of the demons that might follow him out of Ireland?"

"I did not want him to spread panic among the people. The sea rolls between us and Ireland; we have time, at least, to prepare for those demons. But when I heard what Bran's folly had led to I knew that it was time indeed for this island to have another King —one of the true line of Beli."

"You have wanted his crown these many winters, Caswallon; ever since he went into Ireland you have plotted to take it. But you need fear neither Bran nor the demons his folly loosed. The Cauldron has been destroyed, and so has our true King, and most of his people with him."

Light blazed in Caswallon's face; was swiftly veiled. "Hard tidings, druid. Yet if so, kin will not strive with kin. War and bloodshed will be banished from this sea-girt isle for ages to come. Your prophecies are as poor as your spells were when you strove against me, old man."

"Are they so? Before you die you will see invaders, Caswallon; bit by bit you and the kings that come after you will have to yield the land. We have been stripped of our young men as a tree is stripped of fruit, and soon the birds of doom will gather; they will never let us grow such another crop. They will attack and attack, and what strength they do not drain our own strife among ourselves will eat up. For you will be but the first of many, bloody, self-seeking plotters. Yet for awhile, if you keep some of your promises, you can give us peace. Reign then, son of Beli; your hour has come. I strive against you no longer."

Caswallon smiled and thanked him, but in the midst of his thanks the other looked around, staring as if he saw the dead bodies for the first time. With a scream of fear and horror he fled, and did not stop until the green wood of Edeyrnion closed round him. For a moment that flight startled Caswallon, then he smiled.

"It is only the boy. My kinsman's page."

So it was. For the druid had gone out of that borrowed body; Pendaran Dyved was back in Dyved.

Caswallon's thoughts turned then to the great funeral and the great mourning that he would make for Caradoc. He was very glad that he had not had to kill his young kinsman; one cannot doubt, either, that he was more than a little glad to have him dead. The druid's prophecies he thrust out of mind; ill-wishers are often wishful thinkers, and this was indeed Caswallon's hour. No ghosts should stand between him and its joy.

And in Ireland, in the gold of the morning, Bran's huge Head bowed itself where no breast was, over the golden dish that held his blood, and great tears dripped down onto Branwen's white sleeping face.

"It is finished," the Head said. "And it is begun."

14

The Birds of Rhiannon

They toiled, those seven men of the Island of the Mighty who were left in Ireland; toiled to build a ship that would carry them home. They soon found that the charred wood of their wrecked ships was treacherous and rotten; nothing that the fumes of the Cauldron had touched could be made serviceable again. They had to go inland, to the forests, to cut trees and these they had to choose with care; there too the Cauldron's searing breath had been. Then they had to drag the logs to the shore; the work was not easy.

They saw no Irishmen; save for themselves that stricken land was deserted, and when their sweat was not running and their backs aching, they too felt like ghosts. So many had fallen; they were so few who were left.

They had no fresh meat; no game was left to be hunted, but some of the ships' stores were still edible. When Manawyddan first sat down to plan the work, Branwen claimed the task of cooking for them. Silence

fell then, a heavy, shocked silence. Out of it Manawyddan said, "Are you sure, sister? Some of us can
cook."

Never since her son's burning had Branwen looked
upon a fire. Whenever she had had to be near one she
had kept her back to it, or at least turned away her
face. But now she said, "I cannot fell trees, brother,
nor shape wood into ships' parts, but here in Ireland I
have learned well how to cook. I will do what I can."

So she did. While the men built the ship she worked
as quietly as once she had in the kitchen of Tara, and
what she saw in the flames only she knew.

Manawyddan thought, *Maybe it is the beginning.
The first step. Maybe now she will come back out of
the past, into the world of living folk.*

Branwen thought, *This much I can do. For this
little while longer I am needed.*

One other thing she did. Near the place where she
cooked, and where all of them ate, she built up a mound
of earth and stones. Upon that mound she set the dish
that held Bran's Head, and round it she wrapped his
cloak, so that he himself seemed to be standing there,
watching over them.

At first that act of hers troubled Manawyddan, but
he did not like to oppose her, and he told himself,
*Maybe this too is a step. She makes a baby of our
brother's head, thinking she does it only for love of
him, but in her heart she longs for a new child.*

And he was glad that the Head showed no signs of
decay; its color stayed fresh and bright as in life, and
the closed eyes looked as if they only dozed. Every day
Branwen washed it and combed its hair, and every
night she took it with her into her shelter.

The day came when the ship was ready; it was a
day when the sun shone weakly, and no wind blew.
Manawyddan said, "Shall we wait here for spring, we

who are too few to defend ourselves if foes come? They may yet, for I think that the winds did not carry that death smoke over all Ireland. Or shall we take the gifts the Mothers have given and set sail, trusting Them to bring us home?"

As with one voice all said, "Let us go home!" But they did not fear the Irish, or trust the sea; the truth was that none of them could bear to stay in that silent land any longer, that land of death.

The seven set sail, and Branwen was the eighth of that company. With Bran's Head in her lap she sat and looked back toward Ireland until the mists came and hid it. Then she bowed her own head and hid her face in the hair of Bran.

Pryderi said uneasily to Manawyddan, "Is she weeping? You would think she would be glad to see the last of that land, where they treated her so cruelly."

Manawyddan said, "Her son was born there, and is buried there; Irish blood flowed in his veins. We are lucky whose love and hate can flow in single channels; not be mixed together."

But his hopes waned as he looked at her. *What has she to go home to? What all of us want is to go back to a place that is nowhere now. To home as we knew it, to an Island of the Mighty that has sat still, unchanged.*

But it would be changed, and forever. The feasts they went to would be filled with new faces or empty places, and Caradoc would sit as lord of them, never Bran. All their comrades had fallen, all their friends and all their foes, and now they were sailing back alone out of that dead ghost world, with her they had fought for, but the heart in her breast was broken. She was only the seared burning husk of that laughing girl who years ago had sailed for Ireland with her lover.

That prize, their only victory, was lost as well as

won. Manawyddan accepted that fact at last, and bowed his own head.

Night found them fog-bound, unable to see their way through the mists, and the hopefulness, the laughter, that had attended their setting out, all gone. Their troubles had come back like homing birds, and all knew at last that they never would get home. Even if their bodies should still reach there, all would be different. There had been so much death that it seemed that all the world should be dead, and their own voices, muffled there in the fog, were like unnatural and irreverent sounds disturbing the quiet of the world's tomb.

Branwen lay with her cheek against Bran's. Once she whispered, "Brother, is this the end?"

For myself I would be glad to rest. But I do not want Manawyddan to die, or his friends. Least of all that boy who is our nephew, and who still has within him so much power to be happy.

In her mind she added those words, though she did not speak them aloud. She had come to think that there was no need to speak aloud to the Head of Bran. And it seemed to her that the Head answered, though she could not tell—since that first night she never had been able to tell—whether its voice came from anywhere but inside her own head.

"I will bring all of you home, small Branwen."

Morning came, and light. Out of the gray waste of waters rose the gray cliffs of Anglesey, the harsh and everlasting rock. But to all of them it looked as warm and inviting as the lighted door of home does to lost children. How they had got there they could not imagine, but they laughed and rejoiced because they were there.

The *Mabinogi* says that they came ashore at Aber Alaw in Talebolyon, that is on the holy Isle of Anglesey. Good indeed it must have been to feel solid land under their feet again, earth that was so nearly earth of the Island of the Mighty.

There was a wood near their landing place. As they stretched their limbs, Pryderi looked toward it and his eyes danced.

"We can go hunting now," he said. "It is glad I would be of some dinner, and it fresh." He tossed his bright head as if defying that dinner not to be caught and eaten, and he smiled.

Manawyddan smiled to see him smile and Branwen smiled at both of them. But her smile was only a way her mouth moved; it had no light.

"Go hunting," she said, "all of you. I will gather driftwood here on the beach to make a fire with. It will be waiting to cook your meat."

But as she said it blackness came over her and for a breath's space the earth seemed to tip beneath her feet. *Fire—fire—will I never have done with fire?*

Pryderi had not seen; he was laughing. "There will be plenty of meat. And it is almost done with cooking you are, Lady."

She was not sure what Manawyddan's gray eyes had seen . . .

He was the first of the hunters to come back, though he did not bring much game. Together they cut it up and made it ready for cooking. They worked together, and the warmth and closeness of that brought back many things. Almost it built a warm and lighted house around her, walls that her mind could cower behind, like a deer hiding from the hounds.

They were many and strong, those hounds. They were within her, not without. Inescapable—bound to pull her down and devour her.

In time the others came back with their game, and she cooked it. She ate with them and sat by the fire. The sun set. Like the face of a dying woman the sky whitened, though here and there red light still stained it, as with the scarlet of fresh blood.

She thought, *Before night comes I must look at the Island of the Mighty, that I have yearned for so long. From this same shore one can see Ireland . . .*

She rose, she looked. To the west lay Ireland, a flame-tipped, darkening mass. To the east, so close that they seemed almost within her touch, lay the pale shores of the Island of the Mighty. Home . . .

She looked, and all her memories came upon her like hail; such fiery hail as volcanic mountains belch forth to blast the fields of men. She was burned from head to foot with memories; they seared her like coals. They were too many and too terrible for one mind to hold, yet like peaks turned to flames by the sunset the worst rose clear.

Gwern, if I had not sent for help, you would still be alive! What matter what happened to my body, that had brought forth its treasure? I had my island, my refuge then, and I did not know it.

Because of her Ireland lay waste, the green isle of her baby's birth. For her the bravest sons of her own island had died; soon women would be wailing there. Were all those dead any less dead, was her misery any less because she had not been to blame? Only what was mattered; what was, and could never be escaped . . .

She cried aloud to the white evening, "Sorrow that is my sorrow! Woe that ever I was born! For the good of two islands has been destroyed through me."

She moaned once, and her heart broke, and she fell . . .

Manawyddan kissed her cheek and closed her eyes. "Sleep may be best for you, beloved, for the world that we grew up in is gone, and you were too tired to help build a new. Sleep and find Gwern again, and our brothers. And maybe even Matholuch can find some new tale to tell, there before Arawn's face. Maybe it can be your comfort at last, not only your shame, that he was a coward. But it is sad my world will be after you, and the light of you gone out of it."

They buried her in a four-sided grave on the banks of the Alaw. Later the waters must have managed to encircle that last bed of her loveliness, for ages after an islet there was still called *Ynys Bronwen*, "Branwen's Isle."

They left what was left of her, as she had left them, and went on . . .

They crossed the Straits of the Menai, and came to the Island of the Mighty. They who had left it in a host thousands strong came back but seven, with no loot and no prize of victory.

On the way to Harlech a huge crowd met them, a crowd of men and women garlanded, yet sad-eyed. Manawyddan felt his heart turn over in his side when he saw them. He had thought that nothing in the world could touch him any more, but it may be that that is true of a man only when he dies. As Branwen had died, and Caradoc.

He asked the nearest man, "What tidings do these garlands mean?" and he had to moisten his lips before he could speak.

The fellow did not know him; he answered as he would have answered any other man. "Caswallon, son of Beli, has been crowned King in Llwndrys."

"But Caradoc—" Pryderi's voice shook; he had liked his cousin, "what of Caradoc, and the chiefs who were left with him?"

Then the seven who had come home heard what had happened to the seven who had stayed behind.

They went on to Harlech, and there was none to forbid them possession of it. It must already have been stripped of its treasures, if any had been left there, and Caswallon was too small a man to need the windy, roofless courts of Bran. They camped there, in that desolation that once had been thronged with folk and splendor. They sat there, and the Head of Bran sat with them, in its dish.

For long Manawyddan sat brooding, and the others waited. It was for him to speak; he was their King now, rightful King over all the Island of the Mighty, as indeed he had been, by all the ancient laws, ever since Bran died. Their waiting was like a sword that they were pressing into his hand. Their obedience commanded him; their silence made him speak.

He said at last, "Caswallon did not break the bonds of kinship. He did not shed Caradoc's blood; he only broke Caradoc's heart. And not even druid sight can foresee the age when men will call that murder."

"What does it matter what we call it?" Pryderi's hand clenched on his sword hilt. "Let us avenge it. We are only seven, but we are seven who came back from such a war as the world has never seen. And I am still a king; the men of Dyved will follow me."

"To what?" said Manawyddan. "We might win. We might take Caswallon by surprise, and I think there are still many who do not love him. But to win we must bathe the Island of the Mighty in blood. I will never do that. All the less, because the Island should be mine, will I do it—a true king never robs his people of peace."

Silence then; silence deep as that bedded in a grave or at the bottom of the sea. Manawyddan broke it; he laughed, a bitter grating laughter that rang through those barren rocky heights of Harlech, and found its only answer in the gray wash of the sea far below.

"I wondered why, when I cut Bran's head off, he bade me bring it to Harlech. Why he did not say to

Edeyrnion. I wonder—that would have been a sad vision to come to a man in his last hour; and a man that so loved his son—" His voice broke.

Silence again, and then out of the depths of that silence came song. The song of birds, sweeter than any sound of earth; finer and more delicate than any music that ever came out of a human throat. That song had all beauty; its gentleness, its peace, were lovelier than the dream of love; than the cold white Heaven dreamed of by later men. It had the magic of Gods that never condemned, never bade or forbade, but lapped all in the music of their measureless charity; Gods who left man to burn himself until his eyes were clear enough to behold the wonder and peace of their gardens; to do what only oneself can do, and break his own bonds.

Three birds were singing, and they were still far away across the sea, yet by some strange sudden lengthening of their vision, the men on Harlech saw them coming; saw them plain and clear. A gold bird, a white bird, and a green bird, circling, with shining feathers, in the sun.

Pryderi caught his breath sharply. "The Three Birds of Rhiannon, my mother! All she brought with her out of her own world. They are hardly ever seen. I saw them once, and I little; I saw her kissing them, in the dawn."

And the Head of Bran opened its eyes and said quietly, where it sat in its dish, "You have decided as a King should decide, Manawyddan my brother; and as perhaps only you would have decided. Now for seven days we will feast here in Harlech, as we used to do, and my Head will be as pleasant company to all of you as it ever was when it was on my body."

For seven days the Birds sang, and for seven days the tired men feasted, and it seemed to them that all

Harlech's old splendor was upon it, and they were happy there with Bran their Lord. All the evil that had happened was like a dream that they had wakened from, and troubled them no longer. Their plates and their drinking horns seemed always to be full, though how they were filled none knew. That feast was called by later poets the Entertaining by the Noble Head, and to none of the guests who enjoyed his plenty did it seem strange or sad that Bran's body was not there. He himself was, and that was enough.

Six of those seven did not think at all; but Manawyddan thought. Sometimes in the night, while the others slept, the sons of Llyr talked long.

Once Manawyddan said, "Why could you not help Branwen, brother?" And the Head replied, "I tried. But I could not break through the hot cocoon of pain that wrapped her; she was past shock or comforting. Nobody can love too much, but it is in our blood to love one person too much. So our mother dark Penardim loved Llyr our father, so I loved Caradoc, so Branwen loved her baby. And for her there was most excuse of all, our little sister whom I sent from us to spend those dark years in the pit."

"Could not even the Birds have helped her? They for whose loan you must have asked Rhiannon in her dreams?"

"No. They are fledglings of that race whose song takes away the pain of death, so that the dead go down happily to Arawn. They hold none back from rest."

"And she needed rest." Manawyddan sighed.

"As do all of you, whose minds are worse wounded than your bodies; who have seen and borne things that no men have undergone before you. Even on Pryderi there might have been shadows. But you seven I can heal here on earth; when you wake again to your memories you will have strength to bear them."

"You sound as if we were dreaming now."

"Who can be sure when he dreams and when he wakes? What you know now is good; be content."

Another time Manawyddan said, "There is one thing I should like to know, brother, though I suppose it does not matter. You should know, you who have one foot in this one world, and one in the next."

"I have no feet at all, I no longer need them. But I will answer your question if I can."

"It is this. How have the Gods got along without the Cauldron?"

"They never lost it," said Bran's Head.

Manawyddan stared hard at the Head, then scratched his own. "How can that be? I never could see how Llassar and his woman could have had power to steal that Cauldron, yet it is certain that they got Something that had power."

"It was the Cauldron," said the Head, "and it was not. Perhaps I cannot make you understand, you who still have your whole body, but nothing is ever so solid as it seems. Everything that is is many-layered, and each eye that sees a thing sees only part of it—and that a part that no other eye can see. Kymideu Kymeinvoll and Llassar stole the Cauldron *they* saw—not the one the Gods see. The true Cauldron is too fine for earth; it sits unharmed where it has always sat, throughout the ages. What Evnissyen broke was only a blasphemy and a mistake."

"You are right, brother. I do not understand you."

"It is simple," said the Head. "We are never destroyed, though we have all had many bodies that were. And it is the same way with the Cauldron, that never should have had an earth-self in the first place. Sleep now, brother."

A thought struck Manawyddan. "Can you sleep?"

"I need no sleep, who am beyond weariness, and all

the bonds of time and space. When you sleep I go to our parents and our brothers and to Branwen. I am with my son also, my son whom I helped to bring to death, as I led so many of our people to death, because I wanted him to wear my crown. It alone is lost, my brother, and it, in the sense in which I wanted it for Caradoc, was only a trinket after all."

"I could have told you that while you were alive." Manawyddan only thought that, but the Head could hear thoughts. "But then you would never listen. Now that there is less of you, you seem to have more sense."

"Indeed I had to listen," said the Head, "for many a time you would not let me get out of it. But that too is over; it is not about crowns, or any other trinkets that we will bicker again, Manawyddan my brother."

On the seventh day the Head said, "It is time for us to go."

They stared at it in fear. "You will not leave us, Lord?"

"Not yet. We will go to Gwales in Penvro, and there we will feast for eighty days."

They did not question him further. They did not mind leaving Harlech, so long as he was with them; it seemed to them that they had been there seven years, though every hour of that seven had been happy. They set forth, carrying his Head in its dish; and the Birds of Rhiannon flew before them, singing.

They came to Gwales, perhaps now called Gresholm, the Pembrokeshire isle that lies farthest out in the gray murmuring sea. Upon Gwales they found a fair and kingly hall awaiting them; no man or woman was in it. Three doors it had, and two stood open; one faced toward green Penvro, and the second upon the gray-green sea.

"Do not open the door that is shut," said the Head

of Bran. "Not now. The time must come when one of you will, but then my Head will begin to decay and the memory of all your woes and losses will come upon you, and you will be back in the world of men."

"Indeed, Lord," begged Pryderi, "please tell us which of us is going to open that door and kill you all over again, and we will kill that idiot first."

"Then you might stay here dreaming all your lives," said the Head, "and I will neither have that nor bring death upon any more of my men." And the Head looked very straight at Pryderi, and Pryderi looked the other way.

Days came and went, blue and golden, and after each day night came, like a tame dark bird alighting gently upon the hand. And still those Seven feasted and were happy, more at peace than the wholly waking ever are.

And his spies bore word to Caswallon, who had grown uneasy when he heard that Manawyddan and his men were at Harlech, that royal seat that many still held in loving awe.

"They sit in a fisherman's hut, Lord, a place that they found all tumbling down and deserted. They drink spring water and gather seaweed to eat, and they laugh and babble like children. They are all mad, Lord."

Caswallon smiled. "There is nothing to fear from them, then."

So in death Bran the Blessed guarded his men better than he had in life.

At night he and Manawyddan still talked. In after-years, Manwyddan tried to remember those talks, that then seemed lost in a moon-silvered fog.

Once, he knew, he had said, "Nissyen and Evnissyen. Why were they so different, those two sons of the curse?"

Bran's Head had answered, mellow thunder out of

that glowing fog, "Both of them were parts of an Immortal, and Nissyen is not such a part of it as ordinarily is born again into a body of our world. But he chose birth, he came back into this schoolroom that he had outgrown, to keep Evnissyen from doing too much harm."

"Indeed," said Manawyddan, "I cannot see what harm he ever managed to keep Evnissyen from doing."

"He did much," said the Head. "He kept you and me from going to war with each other instead of with Ireland. And he made Evnissyen, whose only power was hate, love him, so that in the end the boy broke the bonds that he had been forging upon himself throughout the ages, and sacrificed himself to save us."

Manawyddan sighed. "Seven of us he saved—only seven . . . Our mother should have let our father die."

"Do not blame her," said the Head. "He had to come. Such as he are part of the world's growing pains."

"You make him sound like something a baby must have cut its teeth on," said Manawyddan. "But he has broken most of our teeth, and to me it always seemed that he was doing the chewing, not we."

"Change will always bring forth twins," said the Head. "Good and Evil. We were born in times of great change, that for my own ends I tried to hurry. And change that comes too fast brings about a triple birth: Hatred and Fear and Strife. Now even I cannot tell in what age peace will come again or tumult end."

"You are not encouraging, brother."

"I am not encouraged. In the darkness that comes man will twist and disfigure both himself and those bastard Gods born of his reaching toward the Unknowable."

Another time the Head said, "Indeed it is not much use to try to make the world clean, as Beli tried and for awhile I tried, unless each person will try to make himself or herself clean. Change that is effectual must come from within the hearts of men; force is an ill broom to sweep anything clean with."

"So we were always taught, brother."

"Maybe we were not taught it well enough. Yet in teachers lies the world's only hope. Force should be used only to keep one man from hurting another; to give teachers peace in which to teach. Both governments and Gods will forget that, though the Gods, being shrewder even in their corruption, as the less material always must be, will always know that the One is all that matters. The individual, whoever or whatever he is. For is not each of us one? Alone, trapped in his separateness?"

"Nothing could be truer than that." Manawyddan sighed. Loneliness—sometimes he woke enough to fear it.

The Head went on. "But governments will think that only masses of men matter, that one individual exists only to make his image like to another, and it is then, when man, maker of governments and of man, sick of his corrupted Gods' cruelty, sets governments above them, that his hour of greatest peril will come. For then his own skills and knowledge, grown Godlike, will turn against him."

"May the Mothers be with him," said Manawyddan. Later he wondered what they had been talking about. Often in those night watches the Head used words strange to him; at the time he understood them, but in the morning their meaning would be gone.

That feast at Gwales was a beginning and an end. The end of the reign of the Children of Llyr, of that fabulous early world that for a generation longer Math the Ancient kept alive in Gwynedd. What it began is not yet finished; yet many mysteries lie between that time and ours.

Once again in the night Manawyddan woke, or thought he woke; perhaps he only dreamed. And in the silver twilight he saw the Head of Bran his brother staring into space, and heard the great voice say, deep and sonorous as the voice of earth:

"Again I shall be the Keeper of the Cauldron. Yes, my Head shall sit in a castle beyond the rainbow river that girdles earth and there order life and birth, and the age-old struggle between Life and Death his brother. For those two brothers of mine and of all men's were born in one hour, though Life is the elder, and both the predestined victor and the predestined prey."

Manawyddan started to ask what the Head meant, but as his lips were opening, a feather of sleep, the dark bird, brushed his face . . .

Indeed, that meaning was always hidden, and now seems lost. But one tale whose teller seems not yet to have heard of the Grail tells how a young hero who should have asked a question and did not came to a Castle of Wonders, and saw there a Bleeding Head upon a tray and a Bleeding Spear.

The Spear of Christ's wounding—or of Bran's?

There are many worlds, and maybe when the reign of the Ancient Harmonies ended upon earth, those Keepers of the Mysteries who had guarded them in the next world above ours passed on, and made Bran the Blessed their heir. For all Bran's mistakes had sprung from love, and at last he had understood himself, and therefore had won as much wisdom as man can, and was ready to become a God.

That would explain much; even why that demon brother of the Lords of Life is said to have crept about invisible, slaying men under the very noses of Arthur's knights. For death is necessary to make room for life. He sounds more like Caswallon than Evnissyen, but Caswallon may have taken Evnissyen's place as the

Destroyer. For one was an individual and the other the beginner of a type and of an age. The son of Beli has slithered snakelike through the centuries, growing ever blacker. Greed is his God, so he is cheaper in his guilt than Evnissyen, who never seems to have cared for gain.

But these things can only be guessed at; never known.

In Caswallon's earthly realm time passed. Above Gwales the second golden moon grew round and passed into darkness. The third rose, slim and horned and shining, began to grow round. The eightieth day came and the eightieth night, and Heilyn, son of Gwyn, woke while his comrades slept. He saw the darkness fade, he saw the two doorways rise out of it, long and pale. He saw the third door, the closed door, appear between the walls, heavy and brown and richly carved, blocking out the dawn.

He was a man of inquiring mind, the son of Gwyn. Whenever there was anything he did not know about, he wanted to find out about it at once. That quality, like fire, can do good work or bad work. Without it man would have got nowhere; with it, many a man has got himself into places he would have given a great deal to get out of.

Heilyn looked at the door, and it seemed to look back at him. To say, *"You cannot see through me. You cannot be sure what is on the other side of me. I am like blindness; I shut you in . . ."*

Heilyn stared at it. He thought, *I could open you. I will not, because it would not be wise. But I could . . .*

The door seemed to jeer at him, as one boy thumbs his nose at another. *"You would never dare. You are afraid of what the Head said would happen. Are you sure it said that? How could a Head talk? Are you sure of anything?"*

He looked toward the Head, but it did not look back at him. The dawn shimmered faintly in its eyes, that might have been looking wisely into the mysteries of space, or might have been only glazed.

He felt suddenly dizzy, uncertain of himself and all things. He sprang up, as if by action to drive uncertainty away. He faced that taunting door; it at least was solid, real.

"By my beard," he said, "I will open this door and see if what is told about it is the truth."

He strode forward; his feet moved and then his hand moved; found that hard solid wood . . .

And then bells seemed to be pealing all around him; wild sweet elvish bells. His comrades started up; he saw their white staring faces, heard their shocked voices. And under his hand was nothing but air. He saw a rude wall with a gaping hole in it, and recoiled.

They all saw; saw what that wall had hidden. The dawn-lit sea and the shores of Cornwall; the mouth of the Henvelen, where it poured into that sea. And sea and sky and river looked as gray as death.

The peal of bells ceased, and they heard the last faint echo of a song. They looked up and saw the Birds of Rhiannon flying away from them, white and green and gold in the drab heavens.

They looked around, and saw no splendid hall, but a fisherman's bare hut. One cried, "Where are we?"

Of all the riches and beauty that had seemed to surround them, only one golden dish was left: the dish that held the Head of Bran. That Head turned its eyes a little now, toward Manawyddan, and smiled with graying lips. For a breath's space the face was still Bran's face, Bran himself was in the eyes and the smile. And then the eyes closed, and the Head slid slowly sidewise, like a ball dropped from a child's hand. It lay on its side in the golden dish, in the midst of the clotting blood, one gray livid cheek bedabbled and upturned . . .

A thin wind blew through the hut, a wind sharp as a sword, and as cold as death.

"It is finished," said Manawyddan. "We are back in our own world. And it is a world without you, Bran my brother, and without almost all that we have ever loved."

In sorrow they left Gwales, that gray place that had been rainbow-bright, and in sorrow they set their faces toward Llwndrys and the White Mount.

Their hearts were dead in their breasts, as dead as the Head they carried, forever silent now in its golden dish. Spring was coming, but they were desolate as naked men wandering in the cold of winter. In that black awakening it seemed to them as though all the dead had died but yesterday, and they grieved for them, and most of all for Bran their Lord.

They came to the White Mount, where now the Tower of London stands, and they buried the Head there, with its face toward Gaul, and the Triads call that the Third Good Concealment. For so long as the dead face of Bran looked toward the continent no invader might set foot upon the Island of the Mighty. So much power to bless had he, even in death, Bran the Blessed, son of Llyr whom dark Penardim had loved. The digging up of that Head is called the Third Evil Uncovering; Arthur dug it up in his young pride, ambitious to hold the Island of the Mighty by his own strength alone, without the help of the ancient mighty dead.

Caswallon must be given credit for doing nothing

to hinder that burial, for he must have known of it. But then Caswallon was never the man to throw away an advantage.

When it was done, Manawyddan said, "We must go on now. If we could reach a good place and stop there forever, that would be good indeed. But that never can be. Nothing can stand still for long; what does not go forward must decay."

His face was sad as he said that, he who was no longer young, and who must go forward alone. But the others suddenly remembered people who might still be alive; people who might be glad to see them. Light came into their faces; the faint stirring, as of plants that sought to put forth new roots. Pryderi sniffed the air like a young hound; eager-eyed he faced westward, toward Dyved.

"I will go home," he said. "To my mother and my people, and to golden Kigva, my woman." He strutted a little. "Maybe I will beget a son. Men just back from war often do. It is a good time for it."

Some of them laughed. Even Heilyn grinned, he who since he opened the forbidden door had been almost as silent as the dead.

Manawyddan said, "Any time is a good time for that." He thought, *It is hard to be left behind, a man, when your kin have joined the Gods. To have none to work with or for.*

He who always had worked with Bran henceforth was to work alone. In little daily tasks he might have plenty of help; in great struggles none. That much was true; but how much work awaited him in that new world into which he was going, how little of it would be for himself alone, he could not yet dream. Now he thought that his loneliness would last as long as his body. But that tale is told in the Third Branch of the

Mabinogi. The Second Branch ends with the burying of the Noble Head.

SO FAR, THE TALE OF BRANWEN AND OF THE CAUL-DRON; OF THE GREAT WAR AND OF HOW THE SEVEN CAME BACK FROM IRELAND.

ABOUT THE AUTHOR

Although it came from the Fourth Branch of *The Mabinogion,* THE ISLAND OF THE MIGHTY, by Evangeline Walton, was the first book to be published. This event occurred some thirty-odd years ago, to great critical acclaim. Commercial success did not match the cheers of the reviewers—perhaps due to the original title, *The Virgin and the Swine*—and the rediscovery of Miss Walton's remarkable talent had to await the publication of Ballantine Books Fantasy series.

Since Miss Walton had already completed the writing of the Second Branch (THE CHILDREN OF LLYR) and the Third Branch (THE SONG OF RHIANNON), these two volumes were the next to appear. Finally, to complete the tetralogy, the First Branch (PRINCE OF ANNWN) was published in 1974.

It is a tribute to Miss Walton's talent as a writer that despite the checkered publication of these volumes, the tetralogy as a whole encompasses a sustained emotional drive, starting with the innocent adventures in PRINCE OF ANNWN, when the world was young and simple, to the gaunt tragedy of THE CHILDREN OF LLYR and the homely heroism of THE SONG OF RHIANNON, climaxing in the towering epic that is THE ISLAND OF THE MIGHTY.

Miss Walton makes her home in Arizona.

DEL REY SCIENCE FICTION CLASSICS FROM BALLANTINE BOOKS

CHILDHOOD'S END, Arthur C. Clarke	27603	1.95
FAHRENHEIT 451, Ray Bradbury	27431	1.95
HAVE SPACESUIT, WILL TRAVEL, Robert A. Heinlein	26071	1.75
IMPERIAL EARTH, Arthur C. Clarke	25352	1.95
MORE THAN HUMAN, Theodore Sturgeon	24389	1.50
RENDEZVOUS WITH RAMA, Arthur C. Clarke	27344	1.95
RINGWORLD, Larry Niven	27550	1.95
A SCANNER DARKLY, Philip K. Dick	26064	1.95
SPLINTER OF THE MIND'S EYE, Alan Dean Foster	26062	1.95
STAND ON ZANZIBAR, John Brunner	25486	1.95
STAR WARS, George Lucas	26079	1.95
STARMAN JONES, Robert A. Heinlein	27595	1.75
TUNNEL IN THE SKY, Robert A. Heinlein	26065	1.50
UNDER PRESSURE, Frank Herbert	27540	1.75

ANNE McCAFFREY